'R RETURN

2 3

R.26

"But Adam needs Super Mommy."

Laura's voice cracked, sending a glass shard of pain through him. How was she ever going to move past the fact that he'd done this to their child? Even assuming Adam returned home safe and sound—and he refused to consider any other possibility—how were they going to move forward as a couple?

He asked slowly, "Do think you'll ever forgive me for all of this?"

She stared across the dark interior of the car at him a long time before she answered. "I don't know. After you lied to me in Paris and then spent the past year knowing you were living under an assumed identity and never told me, I don't know how I'm going to trust you again."

If only he could remember why he'd deceived her in Paris! For the first time, he regretted not really trying to work with the doctors who'd attempted to help him regain his memory.

"Now what?" Laura asked.

What indeed.

Dear Reader,

I cannot tell you how much fun it is to get to revisit a few of my favourite characters of all time, and to get to write about babies and children again, all in one book! I was absolutely thrilled when I was asked to write another book in the Top Secret Deliveries series. Thanks so much to you for supporting these books and giving me and my fellow authors an opportunity to play in this universe again.

There's nothing quite as powerful as the love of a parent for their child, and it was a challenge to combine this with a grown-up love story and a tale of suspense and danger. Thankfully, Nick and Laura knew exactly how they planned to proceed. It seemed like every day when I sat down to write, certain I knew what was going to happen in that day's work, those two up and took me in some completely different direction altogether.

So, I take no credit for this book. This is truly Nick and Laura's story. I was just the typist along for the ride. I hope you enjoy it as much as I did.

Happy reading!

Cindy Dees

The Spy's Secret Family

CINDY DEES

MILLS & BOON®

First published in Great Britain 2012
by Mills & Boon, an imprint of Harlequin (UK) Limited.
Large Print edition 2012
Harlequin (UK) Limited,
Eton House, 18-24 Paradise Road,
Richmond, Surrey TW9 1SR

© Cynthia Dees 2011

ISBN: 978 0 263 22993 6

AudioGO   1 3 APR 2012

CINDY DEES

started flying aeroplanes while sitting in her dad's lap at the age of three and got a pilot's license before she got a driver's license. At age fifteen, she dropped out of high school and left the horse farm in Michigan where she grew up to attend the University of Michigan. After earning a degree in Russian and East European Studies, she joined the US Air Force and became the youngest female pilot in its history. She flew supersonic jets, VIP airlift and the C-5 Galaxy, the world's largest airplane. During her military career, she travelled to forty countries on five continents, was detained by the KGB and East German secret police, got shot at, flew in the first Gulf War and amassed a lifetime's worth of war stories. Her hobbies include medieval reenacting, professional Middle Eastern dancing and Japanese gardening.

This RITA® Award-winning author's first book was published in 2002 and since then she has published more than twenty-five bestselling and award-winning novels. She loves to hear from readers and can be contacted at www.cindydees.com

This book is for Shana Smith
because it absolutely, positively
couldn't have happened without her.
Truly. You're the best!

Chapter 1

Why wasn't he dead?

Nick stared up at the featureless white ceiling of his hospital room as the beeping of a heart monitor punctuated the panic flowing through his veins. Why hadn't they killed him? Why five years of captivity instead—in a shipping container, on a cargo ship, floating around in international waters?

And why couldn't he remember what came just before his kidnapping? The doctors told him he'd sustained a serious head injury at some point during his incarceration. Whether a captor had hit him during an interrogation or he'd fallen during one of the massive open-sea storms that had tossed him like a cork inside his steel prison, he had no recollection.

He coughed thickly. Supposedly, his pneumonia was mostly under control now. It had been touch and go there for a while. But the worry lurking in his nurses' eyes had eased in the past day or so. He gathered he was out of the woods, which was good news.

They were still working on clearing his body of various other infections and trying to restore normal function to his digestive tract. The only way he was putting on weight was via the massive calorie infusions running through his IV.

They'd cut his dark hair and shaved off his matted beard, revealing the unnatural paleness of his usually olive complexion. The psychiatrists said he might never remember the lost time, a memory gap spanning approximately two years prior to his capture and the first three years or so of his imprisonment. Funny how the shrinks were trying so hard to retrieve those memories and he was trying equally hard *not* to retrieve them. Absolute certainty vibrated ominously in his gut, warning him that whatever lurked in that black hole of lost time was best left there.

Was whatever he'd forgotten the reason he was still alive? Had his captors been waiting for him to remember something? Or was there some other, more sinister reason that someone had been hell-bent on imprisoning him?

Maybe he was just being paranoid. Although it wasn't paranoia if someone was really after him. Even now, he expected his keepers to burst into his hospital room and haul him back to his box. The idea actually made a certain sick sense. If his captors had orders to keep him alive and he'd gotten too sick to treat on the ship, they could've cooked up this whole rescue ruse to fatten him up and get him healthy enough to toss back in Hell.

Laura Delaney—the woman who'd rescued him from his metal prison and one of the only faces he remembered from the lost years—claimed the two of them had been lovers before he'd disappeared. She'd introduced him to a little boy who looked so much like him it was hard to discount her story that he was the child's father. He desperately hoped it was true.

She was an extremely attractive woman. It wasn't difficult to imagine dating someone like her. But was she for real? Or was she part of his captors' evil head games? Was she here to trick him into revealing whatever secrets his subconscious was guarding so fiercely?

If only there was someone he could trust, really *trust*, to tell him what was real and what was not.

And then there was the troubling fact that he knew for certain his name wasn't Nick Cass. Nor had he grown up entirely in Rhode Island. But Laura apparently believed both to be true. He must've told the lies himself.

But why? If he and Laura were lovers like she claimed, why hadn't he told her his real name or the most basic facts about his past? Why the deception?

Everywhere he turned, there were only questions and more questions. Frustration sang through his blood as sharply as his secret hope that his freedom, at least, was real. But he dared not share that hope with anyone. Not until he knew if anyone at all was telling him the truth.

Laura paused outside the hospital room, steeling herself not to react to Nick's emaciated state. It wasn't his fault he looked fresh out of a Nazi concentration camp, and he didn't deserve to see her cringe at the sight of his skeletal frame, hollow face or his shadowed blue eyes. God, his eyes. The haunted look in them was terrifying. Would he carry it with him forever?

The shrinks doubted he would recover the years stripped from his memory. But they felt he should recover enough to be a functional member of society once more with time and counseling. He *should* recover. Not he would.

At this point, she didn't care if his memory ever came back. She just wanted *him* back. The man who'd swept her off her feet in a whirlwind romance in Paris. The man who'd captured her heart and taught her what true love could be. If even part of that amazing man came back to her, it would be better than the hollow shell of a man on the other side of the door. She vowed to be grateful for whatever piece of him survived his ordeal. It was surely better than having no part of him at all. The past five years of waiting and wondering had been pure hell.

She knew he wasn't convinced yet that his rescue was real in spite of that first night of freedom they'd shared. They'd gone to her estate, where he'd bathed and eaten. Then she'd made love to him with all the pent-up passion and relief in her soul.

They'd both cried that night. She'd interpreted his tears as a cathartic release, but she'd been wrong. The shrinks told her he believed that night to have been some sort of elaborate torture by his captors to taunt him with what freedom would be like. Apparently, he'd been crying because the idea of going back into his box after what the two of them had shared had finally broken him. *She'd* broken him.

The man hadn't even known who she was, and she'd been so caught up in her euphoria at finding him that she'd never slowed down enough to realize how lost he'd been. Guilt at her thoughtlessness rolled through her. She'd always been a take-charge, full-speed-ahead kind of person. But that tendency had hurt the man she loved. Part of his paranoid state now was her fault. When would she learn to rein herself in? Had her impulsiveness cost her his trust forever?

She took a deep breath and pushed open

the door. "Hey, handsome. How are you feeling today?"

"You're back." The abject relief in his voice broke her heart a little. What he clearly meant was, "So I get to live another day in this beautiful illusion? Thank God."

"The doctors say you can go home soon. You'll still need around-the-clock medical care, but I can hire nurses to look after you."

Terror flashed in his eyes at the mention of leaving the hospital.

She pretended not to see it and asked lightly, "Do you think when you actually come home to live with me and Adam you'll believe all of this is real? That you're free and you have a family?"

He answered slowly, "I don't know. I hope so."

Hey, progress! He'd spoken of his feelings. Maybe he'd finally accepted that he was not living in a dream or a terrible trick. She picked up his bony hand and cradled it in hers. It had been so strong once, so capable of giving her pleasure, so confident in its gestures. She murmured, "I love you, Nick. If you believe nothing else, please believe that."

"Even if you're lying, the notion makes me happy."

She smiled down at him. "Give it some time. Give *me* some time to prove this is real."

He shrugged. "It isn't like I have any choice. I'm along for the ride, here. So far, it's a great dream."

She smiled bravely while the knife twisted in her gut. "You'll be on your feet and kicking up your heels in no time. You'll be able to do whatever you want."

And please God, let that include staying with her and Adam. Their son desperately needed a father, and she desperately needed the man she loved. Yes, she hadn't seen him in five years. And yes, he might be an entirely different person than the one she fell in love with way back then. But surely, at least part of the intelligent, passionate, confident man who'd swept her off her feet was still in there, somewhere.

"How can you possibly be real?" he asked reflectively. "You're too perfect."

She laughed lightly, praying her panic at his declaration wasn't audible. "I'm far from perfect. Trust me."

"Trust. That is the thing, isn't it? Who will trust whom first in this little chess game?"

"This isn't a game, Nick. You're free, you're going home soon and I love you. That's the God's honest truth."

He made a noncommittal sound, and his cobalt gaze slid away from hers.

He really did have to give his captors credit for playing out this farce to the hilt. Six weeks since his "rescue" and still no hint of tossing him back in his box. He gazed around the plush bedroom suite, decorated in dark woods and deep, comforting colors. It was a far cry from his former prison. Hard to believe he actually caught himself missing the container's bare metal walls now and then. After a while, its confines had felt safe. Comforting. A steel embrace that kept out worse horrors.

He supposed if he had to trade one cage for another, this one wasn't bad. It was warmer and softer, and definitely had better food. The hallway door opened and Laura slipped into the room, wearing a slim wool skirt and a silk blouse that clung to her elegant curves in all the right places. Her cheeks were pink and her eyes bright. He added better-looking captors to his list.

In all fairness to her, she'd been nothing but kind and loving to him since she'd opened his box and let him out. She really was a delightful woman, witty and warm, with a quick smile that made her impossible to resist. And she was a devoted mother.

She moved to his side, and he closed his laptop. Yet again, his unreasoning fear at what lurked in his past had prevented him from typing in his real name to an internet search engine. Just a few simple keystrokes, and he'd finally know what monsters lurked in the recesses of his mind. But his terror was just too great. He'd sat there for an hour with the damned computer in his lap and never managed to type a single letter.

Leaning over the chair, Laura kissed him warmly. He didn't find it hard to believe that he'd loved her once. The only thing keeping him from giving in to serious attraction to the woman was the prospect of losing her. He figured as soon as he fell for her, that would be when the rug got yanked out from under him.

"How're you feeling today?" she asked eagerly, almost impatiently.

"Fine. You look about ready to burst. Do you have a surprise for me?" His gut clenched. He hated surprises. He was still waiting for the big, nasty one where his captors swept him out of this paradise and whisked him back to Hell Central.

"I do have a surprise for you, Nick. A good one, I hope. Are you strong enough for a bit of a shock?"

Every cell in his being froze. This was it. Sick heat and then icy cold washed through him, leaving him so nauseous he could hardly breathe. His heart pounded and his breathing accelerated so hard that, in seconds, he was light-headed.

His gaze darted about, seeking escape. Seeking a weapon. Anything to defend himself from the attack to come. His gaze lighted on the window. He could make a dash for it. Fling himself through the glass. It was three stories to the ground. If he went head first, the fall ought to kill him. If nothing else, maybe he'd be hurt so bad they couldn't throw him back in his box. Maybe they'd have to hospitalize him for a few more months.

"I'm pregnant, Nick. We're going to have a baby."

His mind went blank. Ever so slowly, his

brain managed to form a thought. Not a particularly coherent one, but a thought. *What new game was this?*

"Did you hear me?" Laura asked excitedly. "You're going to be a father again."

His brain simply refused to absorb the information. He couldn't find a context to put the words in. Couldn't comprehend the purpose of this new torture.

Laura was laughing. "...too fertile for our own good...first time we made love we got Adam, and now, after that first night you were free, we're going to have another baby...should really be more careful about birth control in the future..."

She was making words and sentences and probably was even stringing them together in some sort of logical order. But he didn't understand a thing she was saying.

He did understand, though, that the hallway door was not bursting open. No thugs had come for him yet. The next few minutes passed with him murmuring inane nothings at proper intervals in response to Laura's babbling joy. And still no one had come.

Could it be? Was this real? Was Laura really pregnant and expecting his child?

Something cracked in his chest. It hurt, but it was a good kind of pain. Was he truly free? Was a life, a future with Laura and his children a possibility? Did he dare hope?

Hope. Now there was a concept.

A baby, huh? His and Laura's. A little brother or sister for Adam. How he'd love to experience all of it—the morning sickness and messy delivery and midnight feedings. Another child to crawl inside his heart and hold it in his or her tiny, precious hands. Lord knew, Adam had already completely wrapped him around his little finger in the short time he'd spent with the boy. Nick said a fervent prayer every night that, even if all the rest of this was a horrible, cruel lie, God would please let Adam be real. He loved the little boy with all his heart.

And now there might be another child for him to love?

Something exploded in his gut with all the bright fury of a fireworks display, burning away everything that had gone before, cauterizing old wounds, and leaving him empty. New. Reborn.

And then he gave that something a name. Joy.

He was free. Really, truly free. The nightmare was over. He surged up out of the chair and wrapped Laura in a crushing embrace. And then, for the first time, he cried for the right reasons.

Laura didn't know what clicked for Nick, but after she told him she was pregnant, he changed. He took new interest in food and exercise and spending time with Adam and generally engaged in life more. He got stronger, and gradually, as her belly grew, the haunted look faded from his eyes. He quit eyeing closed doors suspiciously, and the nightmares seemed to fade.

For a while there, she'd wondered if he was too far gone, if she'd be able to pull him out of the emotional abyss into which he'd fallen. But this baby seemed to have done the trick. She rubbed her rounded tummy affectionately. Things were working out better than she could ever have dreamed. Life was darned near perfect.

Nick stared at the laptop on his desk for the hundredth time. He'd been avoiding the thing for months, ever since Laura had told him she was pregnant, afraid to rock the boat of this new life. Everything was so good for him—for all of them—that he had no desire to do anything to threaten the perfection of it all.

But his curiosity had been building. Maybe it was a sign of his recovery that he was starting to feel the tug of waiting answers. What had happened during those lost years?

Why the lies about his identity? Who'd had him kidnapped and thrown into a box? And why hadn't that person or persons just killed him outright?

Certainty that he did not want to know the answers, no matter how tantalizing they might be, still raged in his gut. Whatever his former life had been, he had no pressing need to resume it. Laura was wealthy enough for them and their children to live in the lap of luxury for several lifetimes. Whoever else he'd left behind in his old life had no doubt made peace long ago with his disappearance and gotten on with their own lives. His return now could only cause disruption and chaos.

But what if his old life, his old identity, came looking for him?

Nah. Surely that had been the whole point of his kidnapping. To turn him into a ghost. Make him disappear for good. As long as he stayed a ghost, made no effort to resume his former life, there was no reason for his past to come looking for him. Right?

The key was to keep a low profile. He closed the laptop with a solid thunk. Nope. Curiosity or no curiosity, he was not going anywhere near his old life.

Chapter 2

Laura sighed. Her perfectly orchestrated schedule for the day had been blown to heck by her obstetrician running nearly two hours late. Not that she begrudged some other patient an emergency C-section. But today, of all days, she'd really needed her doctor to be on time. Because of the delay, she hadn't had time to swing by home and drop off the baby with the nanny before this important meeting with Nick's lawyers.

She winced at the sliding noise of her minivan's side door. Baby Ellie, six weeks old today, was asleep inside, and Laura desperately needed her to stay that way for the next hour. She detached the baby carrier from the car seat base, threw the baby bag over her shoulder and hurried across the parking lot toward the glass and chrome high-rise housing Tatum and Associates, the law firm that would be representing Nick in the upcoming AbaCo trial.

Nick was the star witness for the prosecution. As such, Carter Tatum expected him to come under withering cross-examination by the defense lawyers representing the company's chief of security, Hans Kurtis Schroder. He'd been accused of masterminding a kidnapping and human-trafficking ring using AbaCo ships without the company's knowledge. Personally, Laura doubted Schroder was the top dog in the scheme. He was the sacrificial lamb to protect his bosses.

Today was a coaching session for Nick in how to act on the witness stand. It was guaranteed to be stressful. A part of her that she was trying darned hard to ignore worried that Nick wouldn't be able to handle it. But he'd endured worse. He'd be fine, right?

She stepped out of the elevator and a receptionist ushered her to a plush conference room. Nick smiled and came over to relieve her of baby and bag. Her heart still swelled when he looked at her like that, so tall and dark and handsome. He'd filled out in the past year, lost the gaunt pallor, rebuilt the athletic physique that had first caught her attention in Paris. A shorter haircut than he'd worn then gave him a polished air that felt more Wall Street than European Bohemian. He cut a smashingly gorgeous figure. Her hands itched to get inside his shirt.

As observant as ever, his gaze went dark and smoky. "You are quite a temptation, yourself," he murmured. "Shall we cancel this meeting and go somewhere private?"

She smiled regretfully even as she leaned toward him, pulled in by his magnetic appeal and completely uninterested in resisting it. He stepped forward and his head lowered toward hers. Her breath hitched and she was abruptly hot from head to toe.

A door burst open behind her and several people walked into the room. Nick's gaze shifted briefly to the intruders and then, ignoring them, he completed the kiss. It was a relatively chaste thing, but her toes still curled into tight little knots of pleasure in her Jimmy Choos heels.

"Ahh. You're here, Ms. Delaney. Good. We can get started."

"Sorry I'm late," she murmured. "The doctor was backed up, and I had no time to get home and back here."

Nick cupped her elbow, escorting her to the table and holding her chair for her. "And how's our little angel?" he asked, gazing down at his daughter fondly.

Laura's heart swelled at the adoration in his voice. "Mother and daughter both received clean bills of health." More precisely, daughter was over her mild jaundice, and mother was finally cleared to have sex again.

The past six weeks of abstinence had been murder on her. Nick had just laughed, saying that five years locked up had taught him a great deal of patience.

"Can I get you something to drink, darling?" Nick asked. She shook her head, and his fingers brushed lightly across the back of her neck as he made his way to his own seat. She shivered from head to toe in anticipation of tonight.

Carter Tatum spoke from the end of the table. "This afternoon we're going to try to approximate how AbaCo's lawyers will question Nick. As unpleasant as it may be, I would remind you we're on your side."

Laura, a former CIA operative, had been through training at their infamous Farm, and she highly doubted a bunch of lawyers could throw anything at Nick that she hadn't seen before.

Carter gestured and in short order a trio of lawyers was taking turns rapid-firing questions at Nick. They started with his kidnapping. The Paris police believed he'd been drugged at the Paris Opera and taken to the shipping container in which he spent the next five years. Nick denied remembering any of it. If only she'd gone to the opera with Nick that night, but her CIA partner—and ex-lover, truth be told—had been missing, and she'd been following up a lead.

The lawyers pressed Nick about any enemies who might have paid people to ghost him, and she listened with interest. This was a subject he'd flatly refused to discuss with her. It worried her mightily that whoever'd had him kidnapped was waiting to pounce again. Again, he denied knowing anything.

The next lawyer pushed harder and Nick's shoulders climbed defensively. When the third lawyer pressed even more aggressively for information about Nick's past, he crossed his arms stubbornly and quit speaking altogether. Darn it. That was the same thing he did to her whenever she brought up the subject.

"Water break," Carter announced abruptly.

Laura released the breath she'd been holding. Nick slumped in his chair, his head down. She put a supportive hand on his arm. "Are you okay?"

"Yes," he answered roughly. But his arm trembled beneath her palm, and his jaw clenched so hard he looked about ready to crack a molar.

She suggested gently, "Let's call this for today. We'll come back another time when you're feeling better—"

"We finish it now," he snapped uncharacteristically.

She drew back, startled. Nothing ever flustered Nick. He was always the soul of gentlemanly composure.

"I'm sorry." He sighed. "I have no past. It's over and gone. My life started anew when you rescued me. This is who I am now. You are my life. You and the kids."

She appreciated the sentiment, but he was going to have to face his past eventually. The psychiatrists had told her repeatedly not to push him, to let him investigate his previous life at his own speed. But it had about killed her to contain her curious nature for so long.

The lawyers' badgering resumed, continuing until Nick finally declared, "Gentlemen, this line of questioning is over. My past is not relevant to the fact that I spent five years in an AbaCo box on an AbaCo ship at the hands of kidnappers in the employ of AbaCo."

Laura stared. It was the first time he'd shown even a flash of the decisive streak he'd had in abundance in Paris.

Carter replied mildly, "AbaCo's lawyers will, without question, go on a fishing expedition into your past in hopes of finding something they can make seem relevant."

Nick scowled. "As far as I know, I never had anything to do with AbaCo before I wound up on that damned ship."

The lawyer sighed. "President Nixon's lawyers had the eighteen-minute gap to explain. We've got your five-year blackout to overcome. Have your doctors said anything more about the chances of you regaining some portion of your memory?"

Nick shrugged. "They think everything's gone for good. I remember Laura's face, and that's it."

"Can't you remember something from *before* your memory loss to give you a clue about who you are and what you do?"

"I know who I am and what I do. I'm Nick Cass, and I spend every waking moment enjoying my family."

The lawyer looked regretful, but said firmly, "You're going to be under oath at the trial, and I guarantee they'll ask you for explicit details of your past. If you won't talk, they'll have investigators dig up everything they can find."

Laura observed closely as Nick's gaze went hard. Closed. He'd never talked with her about his past in Paris before he disappeared, either. What *was* the big secret? She'd lay odds he wasn't a criminal. She'd worked with plenty of them over the years, and he just didn't have the right personality for it. He was too honorable, too concerned about doing the right thing.

The lawyers started up again, asking about Nick's connection to AbaCo. He stuck firmly to his story that he'd never had any dealings with AbaCo that he was aware of, and knew of nothing that would've provoked the shipping giant to kidnap him of its own volition. Nick maintained steadfastly that his had to have been strictly a kidnapping for hire.

Frankly, she agreed with him. Laura tapped a pencil idly on the pad of paper before her. With first his long months of physical and emotional recovery and then the new baby coming, she'd been distracted enough this past year to abide by his wishes to leave his past alone. But she felt an investigation coming on.

Somebody'd messed with the father of her children, and that meant they'd messed with her. Furthermore, that person or persons might still pose a threat to her man. She smiled wryly. Her mama bear within was in full force these days. Must be the baby hormones raging.

She listened with a mixture of anger and sadness as Nick tonelessly described his incarceration. The psychologists said he had completely disassociated himself from his imprisonment and would have to make peace with it in his own time. For now, though, he held the emotions at arm's length.

The lawyers moved on to the night of Nick's rescue. He didn't have a lot to say about it other than his door opened and a man named Jagger Holtz let him out, and Holtz and Laura led him to safety.

The lawyers left alone the events to follow Nick's rescue—his weeks in a hospital recovering from various illnesses and malnutrition, his paranoia, the long silences, his difficulties with crowds and open spaces. None of that would help AbaCo's case, apparently.

Then the lawyers attacked the veracity of Nick's whole story, claiming it was entirely too far-fetched to be true, doing their damnedest to trip him up or get him to contradict himself. The only evidence he had of this supposed capture of his was a grainy video that could just as easily have been faked, and they demanded to know why he had it in for AbaCo.

She was ready to explode herself by the time Nick surged up out of his chair. "Why do I have to withstand this sort of character assassination? I'm the victim here! And now you make me a victim a second time!"

Carter nodded soberly. "You are correct. It's the nature of our legal system that the victim often endures outright assault in the courtroom. *That's* what we're here to prepare you to face."

Nick shoved a hand through his hair. "Why exactly do I have to testify?"

"Because AbaCo will try to convince the jury that the video is faked. The government has to have your direct testimony that the events on the tape are real."

"Other people were there that night. Why not put my rescuers on the stand?" He sent Laura a quick, apologetic look, no doubt at the notion of dumping this mess into her lap. Not that she minded. She'd love to say a thing or two about AbaCo to a jury.

Carter grinned. "AbaCo won't touch Laura with a ten-foot pole. She's a former government agent, which gives her credibility, and they bloody well don't want to give her a chance to vent her righteous fury in front of a jury…. The mother of your child alone and frantic for years? Oh, no. Way too damaging a story for AbaCo."

He omitted the part where the government prosecutors wouldn't put her on the stand because she'd illegally obtained most of the information that led to Nick's rescue. They'd rather not open up that can of worms for AbaCo to pry into.

After his outburst, Nick settled into stoic

silence, refusing to respond to any of the leading and obnoxious questions the lawyers threw at him. No matter what they tried, they couldn't shake him. Laura was proud of him, but she didn't like the way he was hunching into his chair, physically withdrawing into himself. He was approaching overload but too macho to admit it.

Thankfully, Ellie woke up and gave Nick the excuse he clearly needed to call a halt for the day. Laura gathered up their fussing daughter apologetically and adjourned to the minivan to nurse and change her.

Nick came outside a few minutes later and stopped by the van to tell her to drive carefully. With troubled eyes, she watched him guide his sporty BMW out of the parking lot. A worrisome, brittle quality clung to him.

Ahh, well. She would make that all go away tonight. The nanny had instructions to entertain the kids for the evening, leaving her and Nick to enjoy a romantic dinner by themselves in the master suite. Smiling, she turned out of the parking lot and pointed the minivan south toward the rolling hills of Virginia's horse country and home.

Nick drove like a man possessed. Heck, maybe he was possessed. What madness was this to subject himself to cross-examination under oath with as many secrets as he clearly had to hide?

If Laura ever found out he wasn't who he said he was…

She couldn't find out. Period. He had too good a thing going, *they* had too good a thing going, to let anyone mess it up. As appealing as revenge against the bastards who'd held him captive might be, it was a no-brainer that his family came first. He'd made that choice months ago, and he'd had no reason to regret it since.

Someone honked at him. He jerked his attention back to the highway and the traffic streaming along it. He could do this. He could hold himself and his life together. One day at time. One hour or one minute at a time if that's what it took. The only honest and good things in his life were Laura and the kids. He wasn't about to lose them.

As the city turned into suburbs and the suburbs into open countryside, his jumpiness increased. After all that time in a shipping container, he'd have thought he would love nothing more than big, blue skies and broad horizons stretching away into infinity. But it turned out the exact opposite was the case. He'd become so used to living in a tiny, mostly dark space that anything else seemed strange and scary.

The panic attack started with sweaty palms and clenching the steering wheel until his knuckles hurt. Then his forehead broke out in a sweat, and an urge to crawl under a blanket in the backseat nearly overcame him.

As Laura's estate came into view, he stopped the car and parked by the side of the road. He had to pull himself together before he got home and scared her or the kids. He hyperventilated until he saw spots before he managed to slow his breathing. He concentrated on Adam's laughter, on Ellie's tiny perfection, on Laura's warm brown eyes looking at him with such love it made his heart hurt.

Gradually, his pulse slowed. He mopped his forehead dry. There wasn't anything he could do about his sweat-soaked shirt, but hopefully Laura would put it down to the grilling earlier from the lawyers. Relishing the car's smooth purr, he put it into gear.

After keying in his security code he drove through the tall iron gates, as always enjoying the bucolic sight of Laura's prized horses grazing in manicured pastures behind freshly painted oak fences. As he pulled into the six-car garage, he was relieved to see that Laura's van wasn't inside yet.

Mumbling a greeting to Marta, the housekeeper, he hurried upstairs to take a shower. The enclosed shower stall with its rain-heads and steam jets soothed away the last remnants of his panic attack. When he emerged from his dressing room/walk-in closet, he heard Laura cooing to Ellie in the nursery. She was a great mom. It added a whole new dimension to the courageous woman who'd rescued him and spent the past year saving his soul.

He poked his head into the nursery. "Anything I can do to help?"

Laura smiled up at him. "I'm afraid you lack the proper anatomical equipment to provide what Ellie wants at the moment." He gazed at his daughter's silky, dark head nestled against the pale globe of Laura's breast. He might have missed Adam's babyhood—another outrage to lay at his kidnappers' feet—but he was savoring every minute of Ellie's.

"Dinner will be ready in a half hour," Laura murmured. "I've asked Marta to serve it in our rooms."

He nodded and retreated to the other end of the hall to play with Adam. It wasn't that he didn't want to sleep with Laura. Far from it. She was as generous and adventurous in bed as she was in life. It was just that he was still rattled from the interrogation, panicked that his past was about to rear its ugly head and ruin all of this perfection. What had happened during those lost years to make him hide his identity, even from the woman he loved?

"Daddeeeeeee!"

Grinning, he braced himself as Adam launched into the air and splatted against Nick's chest. He caught his son's small, wriggly form against his, savoring the smell of soap that clung to the boy's still-damp hair.

"Did you do anything fun today?" he asked as Adam dragged him over to the corner to play with the toy du jour—Hot Wheels race cars.

Adam described his day in charming detail while the two of them built an elaborate racetrack. With dark hair and blue-on-blue eyes so like his own, Adam bent over the task with concentration far beyond his years.

He was a frighteningly intelligent child and would go far in life if he used his talents to their maximum potential. They laughed together as too tight a turn sent cars shooting off the track and across the room in spectacular crashes.

Lisbet, the English and shockingly Mary Poppins-like nanny, interrupted the crash fest to announce that Adam's dinner, and Mummy and Daddy's, were served. Nick gave his son a bear hug and tickled him until Adam was squealing with laughter before turning him over to Lisbet.

Nick stepped into the private sitting room in their suite and stopped in surprise. The space was lit by hundreds of candles and a white-linen-covered table sat alone in the middle. A red rose in a crystal bud vase sat between the two place settings, and a sumptuous meal was laid out. Marta had really outdone herself. It was some sort of exotic fowl served *en croute*—grouse, maybe. Among other things, the German woman was a Cordon Bleu-trained chef. A real treasure. But then Laura didn't settle for less than the best in any aspect of her life. She'd be as intimidating as hell if she weren't such a genuinely warm and kind person. No doubt about it. He didn't deserve her.

Laura stepped out of her dressing room and his breath caught. She was wearing a little black dress that highlighted her newly slender body, which had already mostly regained its pre-pregnancy shape partly due to long hours with a personal trainer over the past month. Frankly, the additional curves added to her appeal.

"You look ravishing," he announced.

"And you are as handsome as always," she replied as he held her chair for her.

Something within her called to him at a fundamental level, a pull at his soul to protect her and make her happy. It went so far beyond mere attraction he didn't know how to give it a name. Even calling it love didn't seem adequate to encompass his need for her or the bond he felt with her. Maybe it was sharing parenthood of two amazing children.

Or maybe it was the fact that he owed his life to her. He would never forget the sight of her the night he was freed. His own private angel. And then the long months of patiently nursing him back to health, gradually convincing him his ordeal was actually over. Putting up with his unwillingness to face his past. And through it all, her love had been steadfast.

He wondered sometimes if there was anything that could shake her loyalty to him. What was it that lurked so dark and frightening in his past? Was it bad enough to drive her away? It really wasn't something he wanted to find out.

"How are you holding up after being raked over the coals by those lawyers?" Laura asked.

He shrugged. "Today wasn't fun. But I expect the trial will be worse."

She sighed. "It'll all be over in a few weeks, and then we can get on with our lives."

His gaze dropped involuntarily to her naked left hand. She never once hinted at it, but she had to be thinking about marriage and wondering why he never brought it up. The truth was, he didn't know if he was married or not, and the only way to find out would be to investigate those ominous, lost years.

He picked up his water glass—since Laura couldn't drink wine while nursing, he wasn't drinking either—and said, "A toast. To a long and happy future for us and our family."

She sipped her water and then asked reflectively, "Why don't you ever talk about the past?"

He frowned. "I've told you why." *Repeatedly, in fact.*

"I'm concerned that, with all the publicity this trial's going to receive, whoever had you kidnapped five years ago will see you and come after you again."

He swore mentally. He hadn't thought about the publicity. Was there some way to declare a moratorium on filming or photographing him during the trial?

"Talk to me, Nick. Between the two of us, we can beat any threat that comes our way."

A naïve notion at best. "My previous life happened a long time ago in a galaxy far, far away. Let it be."

"The psychiatrists keep telling me to let you deal with your imprisonment and the memory loss in your own time. But I have a gut feeling that your time is running out."

So did he.

Thankfully, she let the subject drop. For now. He had no doubt she would bring it up again, though. And one of these days, she wasn't going to back off. She'd insist they find answers. His throat tightened until he could hardly swallow the delicious food. What the hell was he going to do? His entire being shied away from thinking about the past. What could have freaked him out at such a soul-deep level? He put the problem in a mental drawer and slammed it shut. *Later. He'd think about it later.*

They finished eating, and he changed the music. "Dance with me?" he asked her.

"I thought you'd never ask, Mr. Cass."

Nick held a hand out to her and she took it, rising gracefully to her feet. She wasn't particularly tall, but she made up for it by being impossibly elegant in build. He might not remember meeting her, but he had no trouble understanding why he'd fallen for her the first time around. Or the second time around. He figured falling in love with the same woman twice was proof positive he'd chosen the right one.

She came into his arms, soft and willing and smelling of Chanel No. 5, his favorite. "Have I told you today that I love you?" he murmured as they swayed to the slow jazz tune.

"I do believe you've been remiss in that department."

"My sincere apologies. Perhaps I can show you how much I love you instead?"

She laughed. "I *really* never thought you'd ask that. I was beginning to think you didn't miss making love with me."

"Ahh, sweet Laura. I was only trying to think of your health. I will want to make love to you until the day I die."

"Here's hoping that's a very long time from now."

He smiled down at her. "I don't know about you, but I'm planning to live to be one hundred and fifty years old."

"That sounds like a plan."

They danced in silence after that, letting anticipation build between them. Finally, he turned her in his arms toward the bedroom. Her dress had a long zipper, which he drew down by slow degrees as they went, his fingers dipping inside to relish her satin skin and the inward curve of her back. Gratitude swelled in his heart for whatever fate had brought them together.

For her part, Laura tugged his shirt clear of his trousers and made a slow production of unbuttoning it, kissing her way down his chest button by button. His stomach muscles contracted hard as she approached his belt buckle. Her clever fingers did away with that barrier, and then he was sucking in his breath hard, falling back onto the bed when she pushed him gently. She'd obviously given tonight a great deal of thought, and he was happy to go along with her plans for them. For now, at least.

She took her time, teasing him until his entire body thrummed with terrible tension. Finally he rolled over to return the favor. He kissed every inch of her body, reacquainting himself with it, enjoying the new firmness across her flat stomach, loving the extra fullness in her breasts—and the added sensitivity that came with it. Her soft gasps of pleasure were just as he remembered, the way she arched up into his hands, the fire in her eyes as he stroked her body until it sang for him.

A shadow of fear crossed his mind, but he shoved it away. Nothing must hurt her. Hurt them. He ordered himself to stay in the moment. Focus on the now. "You drive me out of my mind," he muttered against her skin. "I'll never get enough of you."

Moaning as his fingers made magic upon her body, she pulled him down to her impatiently. "Nick," she gasped, "Please. I've waited so long for you. I want you now."

Ahh, always direct, his Laura. "I could never deny you what you want, my love."

Taking into consideration her long abstinence, he entered her gently, stunned at how tight and slick she was. She surged up against him immediately, crying out in pleasure. Her eyes glazed the way they always did when they made love, and he relished the way she bit her lower lip. As if she'd actually be able to hold back the cries of pleasure about to claim her. He withdrew slightly and then filled her again in a single slow stroke. She cried out against his shoulder, shuddering from head to foot.

He smiled down at her. "Let us see just how much pleasure you can stand, shall we?"

He paced himself carefully, driving her farther and farther over the edge. With each climax, her smile became more brilliant, her eyes more limpid, his own pleasure more intense. And the happier he became, the more afraid he became. He drove himself mercilessly, forcing himself not to think of the darkness creeping up on him, holding it back from Laura by sheer force of will.

Finally, when his mental strength was at an end, the battle lost, he gave in to the dark tide sweeping over him, surging into her, driving her over the edge one last time. As they climaxed together, it was so magnificent and terrible that, as tears of joy ran down her face, he wasn't far from tears himself. Tears of sheer terror. The better things were between them, the more certain he was that all of it could end at any moment.

He was losing it. Happiness made him unhappy. Joy terrified him. It was all coming apart before his eyes, his life unraveling because he was too screwed up just to enjoy what they had. But he couldn't shake the sense of something bad approaching, something stealthy and evil. And it was coming for him.

"I love you, Nick." Her gaze was clear, untroubled. She sensed nothing, and she had the finely honed instincts of a CIA agent. Desperate, he ordered himself to hold on. Keep it together. He mustn't lose what little sanity he had.

He rolled to his side, propping himself up on one elbow to gaze down at her. "I love you, too, darling." *Must concentrate on that.* Laura. Love. The darkness retreated a little from his mind. His left hand idly stroked down her rosy body. "Better?" he murmured.

"Spectacular. I feel like a woman again."

He leaned down to kiss her. "You were always a woman. A beautiful one. You're an amazing mother, and it only makes you sexier."

"You're just saying that to be polite."

"No, I'm not." He frowned. "Never doubt your attractiveness. The more sides of you I see, the more attracted to you I am."

"Never change, Nick."

If only. He felt as if he'd been living in a state of suspended animation for the past year. As if time was passing, but he wasn't really living. As Laura drifted to sleep beside him, the darkness pushed forward again, nearly choking him with certainty that this sweet interlude was about to end, and life was about to come looking for him with payback in mind.

Chapter 3

The bedside clock had passed 2 a.m. when Nick gave up on sleep. He slid out from under the covers and dressed quietly, tiptoeing downstairs in anticipation of Ellie's imminent feeding. He pulled a bottle of pumped breast milk out of the refrigerator, warmed it in the microwave and went back upstairs.

Turning off the baby monitor, he sat down in the rocking chair to wait. Sure enough, in about ten minutes, the baby started to stir. He picked her up, inhaling the sweet scent of her. "Good evening, little angel. What say we let Mommy sleep tonight?"

Ellie, a happy and cooperative baby, readily took the bottle from him, snuggling close against his chest with a trust that took his breath away. He loved Laura with all his being, but the feelings that swelled in his heart as he gazed down at his daughter pushed his capacity for love to new heights he'd heretofore had no idea existed. Adoration mixed with protectiveness, hope for her future, and wonder at the miracle of her existence expanded in his heart to make room for his tiny daughter.

He changed her as she grew sleepy and rocked her for just a minute or two before her eyes closed. He laid her down gently in her crib and watched her sleep until it dawned on him that he was standing there grinning like a blessed fool.

Restless, he wandered downstairs. Predictably, his feet carried him to his office. Or more accurately to his laptop computer. He sat down at his desk in the dark and cranked it up. He didn't stop to question what he was doing. It was time.

He typed in the name, Nikolas Spiros, and hit the search button. Skipping the tabloids, he read story after story from the business pages chronicling the tragic mental breakdown of Greece's richest shipping magnate. There were even pictures of him, bearded and wild looking. Abrupt memory flashed of his captors hanging a white sheet in his box and taking pictures of him standing in front of it. Bastards.

According to the articles, he'd been institutionalized at a private facility. Later stories talked about his withdrawal from public life. His wish to live quietly and not involve himself with business affairs. How in the hell could anyone who'd known him have believed that drivel? He'd loved running Spiros Shipping. Had thrived on it. The company had been his life, dammit!

He checked his anger. Nikolas Spiros was dead—or at least resting comfortably in an asylum and happy to stay there.

His shipping company had been sold quietly about a year after his "breakdown." Such a pleasant word for such an unpleasant thing as kidnapping. An entirely new management group had taken over the company. A bunch of Germans. They'd renamed it—

His heart nearly stopped right then and there. Spiros Shipping had been renamed AbaCo. The betrayal of it was breathtaking. He'd been kidnapped and held by his own employees! Had they known who he was? Had he been that bad a boss? Surely not. Morale had been great at Spiros before his memory went black. A sense of family had pervaded the firm. Sure, the work had been hard and times were tough, but he'd prided himself in never laying off an employee and paying as much as he could afford to every single worker. Surely so much hadn't changed after his memories stopped that his employees would have turned on him so violently and completely.

In shock, he researched the financials of his renamed company. Profits were down, but

AbaCo was still in the black. He shrugged. It would have been darned hard not to make money given how financially sound the company had been when he last remembered it. He studied the quarterly earnings reports for the past few years and cracks were definitely starting to show. But nothing that couldn't be corrected with wise and careful management for a few years—

Not his company any more.

At least not in any way that mattered. He had Laura and the kids. And at all costs, this other part of his life had to be kept away from them. The new owners could have Spiros Shipping.

Best to just stay hidden. A ghost.

But how in the hell was he supposed to do that with this trial coming up?

What had happened to Nikolas Spiros? Had he gone mad for real? Had something horrible happened at the shipping company that had driven him over the edge? What would leave such a residue of terror within him?

The walls of his office started to close in on him unpleasantly—which was a first—and he actually felt a driving need to get out of there. He erased his browsing history and shut down the computer before heading for the kitchen.

Pulling on a jacket, he turned off the elaborate security system and headed out the back door toward the woods behind the house. Tonight he didn't feel up to trekking across one of the pastures and challenging his agoraphobia. He'd been taking secret hikes for several months now, trying to desensitize himself to open spaces. It was getting better, but by maddeningly slow degrees.

He'd been walking for a few minutes when the panic attack hit. It slammed into him like a freight train, sudden and overwhelming. He stopped, breathing as if he'd been sprinting, and glanced around in terror. And then something odd dawned on him. This panic attack was different. It was accompanied by a strange certainty that he was being watched. Great. Was he slipping back into the paranoia of the early days, too?

He couldn't help himself. He slid into the darkest shadow he could find and crouched, pressing his back against the trunk of a huge sycamore. He let his gaze roam, his peripheral vision taking in a wide angle view of the woods. The night sounds had gone dead silent. Maybe he wasn't so paranoid, after all. The crickets never lied.

Who else was out here? And why?

The motion sensors at the house would warn of any human-sized intruders...if he hadn't turned the alarm system off before he came out here. He swore at himself. Laura and the kids were unprotected. He had to get back to the house. Get the alarms back on. Protect his family.

He stood up and was stunned to discover his feet wouldn't move. Literally. By sheer force of will, he overcame his panic, ignoring the hyperventilation, ignoring the wild imaginings of being kidnapped again, crammed in another box. His family came first, dammit. He'd die for them!

His stumbling walk turned into a jog, and finally into a full-out run. Whether he was running toward Laura or away from the bogeyman in the woods, he couldn't say. But either way, his long legs devoured the distance with powerful strides and his lungs burned with exertion by the time the mansion came into sight. Its Georgian grandeur was dark. Quiet. Undisturbed.

The silliness of his terror struck him forcefully. His mind was playing tricks on him. It was only his past pursuing him. A figment of his imagination. With a last look over his shoulder into the shadows of the night, he let himself into the house and turned on the security system.

Shaken to his core, he climbed the stairs quietly. No sense waking everyone because he'd had a panic attack. He put his hand on the doorknob to let himself into the master suite, but he couldn't bring himself to enter.

He was still too wired to lie down beside Laura as if everything was perfectly normal.

Instead, he headed for another door farther down the hall. A small, walk-in linen closet. About six feet by eight feet inside, its tight quarters felt like a comforting embrace. He slid down the wall and sat on the floor, his elbows on his knees and his head on his arms. He had to get over this. Get a grip on himself. But how? If anything, he was getting worse, not better.

As understanding as Laura tried to be, she couldn't begin to comprehend what he'd been through, what the past few years had been like. It was his own private hell, and no one could climb into it with him and lead him out. He was lost, and getting more lost by the day. Oh, the shrinks said all the right things, but they had no more clue what he'd been through, really, than Laura did. They had a little more book learning about it, had a list of suggestions to offer out of some counseling text, but their psychobabble was mostly crap.

How could everything be so perfect and yet so screwed up? He ought to be insanely happy. But instead, he was marching at a brisk pace toward the mental meltdown he'd been falsely accused of having six years ago.

There hadn't been anyone in the woods. A deer or some other creature had moved, and the crickets had gone quiet for a minute. He'd flipped out over nothing. So why was his fight-or-flight response still in full readiness? He took several deep, calming breaths, the way the yoga instructor had taught him, breathing out the fear and stress.

It accomplished exactly nothing, dammit.

He sat there, panting in terror for who knew how long when, without warning, the door swung open. He started to surge to his feet when a little voice whispered, "Daddy?"

Nick sank back down to the floor, his heart about pounding through his rib cage. "Hey, buddy. What are you doing up at this hour?"

"I dreamed a bad man was coming for me."

He held out an arm to Adam, who wasted no time climbing into his lap. "No bad man will ever get you. Mommy and I will always protect you and keep you safe."

"Promise?"

"I promise."

"Cross your heart and hope to die?" Adam added.

"Cross my heart and hope to die," he repeated. "Need a pinkie swear on it, too?"

Adam held out his right pinkie finger, and Nick hooked his much larger finger in his son's. They shook on it soberly.

"Why are you in the closet, Daddy? Are you hiding from the bad man, too?"

"I didn't want to wake up you and Ellie and Mommy, and I needed some time to think."

Adam's little palms rested on his cheeks. "Is your heart hurting again?"

Since when were five-year-olds so damned perceptive? "I guess it is, a little. I'm so happy it hurts. I think about all the ways it could go wrong…"

Adam nodded wisely. "And then you're not so happy anymore."

He stared down at his son, but it was too dark to make out his face. "Nothing's going to go wrong, Adam. Not if I can help it."

"Don't be scared, Daddy."

"I won't if you won't. We can be brave for each other. Okay?"

Adam nodded against his chest. They cuddled in the dark for several more minutes, and predictably, the boy drifted back to sleep, his nightmare long gone. Nick stood awkwardly, careful not to wake his son, and carried him back to his rocket-ship bed. He tucked the little boy in and kissed his forehead, memorizing Adam's face in that peaceful moment.

He was going to defeat his own demons if it killed him. No way was he about to let his paranoia bleed over to his children and damage them. And furthermore, his past wasn't going to hurt them, either. He knew what he had to do. And he had to do it alone. Leaving no note that Laura could use to track him down, he treaded quietly back down the stairs, this time being sure to reactivate the alarm from the panel in the garage, and headed out into the night.

Laura woke up to Ellie's fussing amplified through the baby monitor, disoriented at how well rested she felt and that the first light of dawn was peeking in around the curtains. She looked at the clock. Six o'clock? Nick must've taken the 2:00 a.m. feeding, bless him. She rolled over to thank him and was startled to see his side of the bed empty. He hadn't struggled with insomnia for months, now.

Shrugging, she got up, threw on a bath-robe and headed for her daughter. Ellie was hungry, and nursed for longer than usual. Laura carried her into the bathroom and laid her on a big soft bath towel on the heated floor while Mommy jumped into the shower. She dressed herself and Ellie and headed downstairs in search of Nick.

He wasn't in the kitchen watching the financial news and drinking coffee, as was his habit. She strolled through the entire downstairs and didn't find him. Had he crawled into bed with Adam sometime last night? He did that now and then when Adam had a particularly scary nightmare. The boy had had periodic bouts with them ever since a team of killers had broken into the house after Nick's rescue in search of her and Nick. Thankfully, the babysitter had gotten them into the mansion's panic room and locked it down before Adam was hurt or worse. But the incident had left its mark on the little boy.

She headed upstairs and peeked into Adam's room. He was sleeping alone. A low-level hum of alarm started in Laura's gut. She checked the linen closet and Nick's walk-in closet. No sign of him.

She pulled out her cell phone and dialed

his. Not in service? What was going on? She ran down to the garage to check the cars—they were all in their places. The alarm system was still on, too. Where had he gone? He hated being outdoors. It wasn't like he'd have gone for a morning stroll.

Starting at one end of the house, she searched it methodically, checking every place a grown man could possibly hide. Something was wrong. Very, very wrong.

Memories of Paris flashed through her head with horrifying clarity. How he'd just disappeared. No trace. No evidence. No ransom call. Nothing. He'd just been gone. *Please, God. Not again.* She couldn't live through losing him again. Not like that.

An hour later, she was on the phone to the police and local hospitals. Nada. And then she started calling their friends and associates, the early hour of the morning be damned. No one had seen or heard from him overnight. Panic hovered, vulture-like, waiting to close in on her.

Adam came downstairs and didn't help matters one bit by immediately picking up on her stress. The child was far too observant for his own good sometimes. "What's wrong, Mommy? Where's Daddy?"

"I don't know, honey. But there's nothing to worry about."

Adam frowned. "His heart is hurting again."

She turned on the child quickly. "Why do you say that, sweetie?"

"He was in the towel closet again last night."

"When last night?"

Adam shrugged. "It was dark. I had a bad dream and was coming to sleep with you. I heard him breathing funny in there."

"What did he say?" She tried not to sound hysterical but suspected she'd failed when Adam frowned worriedly.

"He promised he'd keep me safe from the bad man. He pinkie swore." The little boy started to cry. "The bad man got him, didn't he?"

She gathered him into her arms. "Daddy?

Are you kidding? He's big and strong and smart. No bad man has a chance against your daddy."

But the bad man had gotten Nick once before. Had history sickeningly repeated itself? Had he been ghosted out of their lives yet again?

Chapter 4

"May I help you, sir?" The receptionist at the swanky Boston law firm was predictably beautiful and efficient.

Nick replied, "I'm here to see William Ward."

"Do you have an appointment?"

"No, and please don't tell him I'm here. It's a surprise." He flashed his most charming smile at her. He wasn't vain about his looks, but very few women could resist him when he turned the charm all the way up.

She simpered something about being delighted to help. He waved off her offer to show him the way and strode down the familiar hallways. A feeling akin to déjà vu passed over him. This place was from another existence, another life, familiar and yet entirely strange to him.

He stepped into Ward's office and the man glanced up. *"Sweet Jesus!"* he gasped, falling back in his chair heavily. "Is that really you?"

Nick closed the door and stepped up to the desk. "You look like you've seen a ghost, William."

"My God. Where have you been? The things they said about you—"

Nick propped his hip on a corner of William's expansive desk. "What *did* my kidnappers say to explain my absence, anyway?"

"Kidnappers?" The lawyer stared, aghast. "The reports said you had a mental breakdown. Had to be institutionalized. There were doctor's statements. Psychological evaluations. Pictures. You looked like hell."

"Lies. All of it," Nick said shortly.

William's shocked pallor was giving way to a sickly shade of green. "Was our power of attorney over your estate illegal, then? What about your signatures on all those sales documents?"

"What documents?"

"The ones signing over your company to the new management group? Were those real?"

"I never signed anything, to my knowledge." *He hoped.* Surely he never would have signed away Spiros Shipping under any circumstances.

It took William a few seconds to quit spluttering and form words. "Please forgive me for asking, I mean no disrespect. But have you been in a sufficiently...alert...mental condition for all of the past six years to know for certain that you never signed any legal documents?"

Nick swore under his breath. God only knew what he'd done during the blackout years. "I'm actually not here to talk about my company. And to answer your question, I was kidnapped and imprisoned for five years. It has taken me most of the past year to recover physically from the ordeal."

The lawyer devolved into a shockingly uncharacteristic bout of mumbling to himself. Poor guy must really be shaken up. Eventually, William collected himself enough to go into attorney mode. "I'm going to need an affidavit from you describing exactly what happened to you in detail. I don't have any idea how we're going to contest the sale of your company. It's going to cause a massive uproar to try to get it back—"

Nick interrupted the man sharply. "I don't want it back. That's not why I'm here."

William stared blankly. "Why are you here, then?"

"I need you to tell me about the last two years before I...disappeared."

"I beg your pardon?"

Nick sighed. "It's a long story, but I've experienced a memory loss as a result of a blow to the head. I need your help to fill in the gap."

"Are you serious?"

"As a heart attack."

William nodded dubiously. "I'll do what I can."

The lawyer started talking and Nick listened grimly. He'd thought if he heard about the lost time it would jog his memory, but none of the names or places or dates rang any bells. His memory wasn't just buried. It was truly gone. The danger of the black hole loomed even larger as the true depth of it became clear to him.

"I can get all these facts off the internet, William. Tell me what I was like. How I was acting."

The lawyer spoke of Nikolas growing bored with running a company that functioned like a well-oiled machine pretty much on its own. Of his forays into ever more dangerous hobbies—skydiving, extreme skiing, boat racing, Formula One car racing. He'd apparently blown through a string of beautiful and ever wilder women as well. He'd become a regular on the pages of the European tabloids. And there'd been the partying. Ward didn't say if he'd dabbled in drinking or drugs, just that the lawyer had been very worried about his longtime client.

Finally, he fell silent.

Nick didn't even know where to begin processing the information dump he'd just received. It was odd to hear about his own life and feel so completely disconnected from it. Nothing the man had described would account for the pervasive terror that was the only thing he'd carried forward from that time. Nick asked grimly, "Was I—Did I…get married?"

William looked surprised. "There were rumors of a quickie wedding just before you disappeared. But I hadn't seen you for a few weeks prior to that. I couldn't say."

Rumors of a wedding? Nick swore under his breath. "Do you know how I came by the Nick Cass identity?"

The attorney cleared his throat. "During

that time, you occasionally preferred to travel under an alias to avoid the publicity and scandal you were generating."

He had no memory of being assaulted by paparazzi. "Where did the fake ID come from?"

William visibly squirmed at that one. "For the record, I arranged no such thing. I put you in touch with a gentleman who was expert at facilitating replacement of lost identity documents. Perhaps he was the source of your… alter ego."

Nick dismissed the lawyer's double-talk with a flick of his wrist. If he was going to keep up the charade of being Nick Cass and no one but Nick Cass, he had to know everything there was to know about the man. Had someone of that name really existed at some point, or was Nick Cass an entirely made-up entity? "I need to get in touch with the fellow who made those documents. I need to know more about the identity he provided for me."

William frowned. "It's my understanding he's no longer in the business. He ran into some legal troubles. Last I heard, he left the country in a hurry. I would have no idea how to get in touch with him."

Damn. Frustrated, Nick moved over to the floor-to-ceiling glass window to stare down at Boston Harbor. His kidnapper surely knew who he really was. But did the people who'd held him captive? Did the powers-that-be at AbaCo? Had it been an inside job, or had his kidnappers merely had a sick sense of humor to have imprisoned him on one of his own ships?

If AbaCo's lawyers penetrated the Cass identity, they would come after him with both barrels, and the sum total of what he knew about his last years before his capture he'd just heard from the man behind him. He turned to William. "Can you recommend a top-flight private investigator to me? Someone thorough and discreet."

"Of course." William looked close to

puking in relief that Nick didn't pursue the fake ID thing any further. As Nick recalled, William had been paid plenty well enough back then that he could darn well suffer a little for the cause now.

"Oh, and one more thing, William."

The lawyer looked up sharply from the sticky note on which he was copying a name and phone number.

"Don't tell anyone you've seen me. Consider this little visit a privileged interaction between the two of us. As far as you know, I'm still sitting in a padded cell somewhere, staring at my toes and drooling down my chin. Got it?"

The attorney frowned. "I understand. Actually, I don't understand, but I will abide by your wishes."

"Thanks, William."

"Will you tell me the whole story someday?"

"If things go well, you'll never see or hear from me again." As the finality of that struck

Nick he made brief eye contact with the attorney who'd been a friend and confidante for many years. "Thanks for everything. You're a good man."

"You, too. If you ever need anything, just let me know. And good luck."

Nick turned and left the office. Good luck, indeed. He'd probably need a bona fide miracle before it was all said and done to avoid the clutches of his past.

He waited until he was back in Washington D.C., leaving Reagan International Airport to drive home, before he called Laura. She had too many scary resources with which to track him down for him to risk calling her any sooner. She would be completely freaked out by now, but he'd had no choice. He had to deal with his past on his own. And after hearing what William Ward had to say about his last years leading up to his capture, it had turned out to be a damned good call to keep Laura and the kids far away from the mess he'd apparently made of his life.

Laura answered her cell phone on the first ring with a terse hello.

"Hello, darling. It's me."

"Thank God, Nick. Are you all right? Are you hurt? Where are you?"

He felt terrible hearing her panic and relief. Good Lord willing, he'd never scare her like this again. "I'm fine. I'll be home in about an hour. There was something I had to take care of."

A pause. "Can you talk to me about it?"

"I'm afraid I can't. But it's handled. No worries." At least he hoped there was nothing to worry about. The P.I. he'd spoken to in Boston had been confident he could find everything that had ever existed on one Nick Cass prior to six years ago. If the man had ever actually existed, Nick would know all about him in a few days.

The cab delivered him to the mansion's front door in closer to two hours than one—there'd been an accident and traffic was hellish. As he stepped inside, Adam shouted a greeting that warmed Nick all the way to his soul. Laura held herself to a walk as she came to greet him, but she squeezed him so tightly it hurt and he thought he felt a sob shake her momentarily.

"I'm sorry, darling. I knew you'd want to go with me, but I had to take care of a piece of old business on my own."

Her muffled voice rose from his chest. "Did you kill anyone?"

"No," he laughed.

"Are we okay?"

His arms tightened convulsively around her. "That's the whole idea. I love you and the children more than life." They stood locked together like they'd never let go of each other for a long time. Finally, he murmured, "Am I forgiven?"

"Of course. I could never stay mad at you. If you say you had to do something, then you had to do it. If you can't talk about it with me, there's a good reason for that, too. And if you say you love me, I believe you."

He tilted her chin up to kiss her. "I am, without question, the luckiest man on Earth to have you."

She stood on tiptoe to kiss him back. "And don't you ever forget it," she murmured.

"Never." Their lips met, and the passion that always simmered between them boiled over immediately. His mouth slanted across hers, and she clung to him eagerly.

"Eeyew! Gross!" Adam exclaimed from the steps above them.

Nick lifted his mouth away from Laura's and smiled up at his son. "For now, you hold on to that thought, young man. But trust me. In a few years, girls won't be nearly so disgusting."

"But Mommy's not a girl. She's a…mommy."

Laura laughed in Nick's arms. "Gee, thanks, kid." She scooped up Adam and swung him around until they were all laughing.

And just like that, life was back to the way it was supposed to be. As Nick followed his family toward the kitchen, he experienced an overwhelming sensation of having dodged a bullet.

The sensation lasted exactly one hour. That was when Carter Tatum called to inform him that he was to appear at a pre-trial hearing in three days' time. Three days for the private investigator to give him enough ammunition to hold off a pack of sharks out to tear him to pieces. It was almost enough to make him reconsider enlisting Laura's prodigious skill with computers to help him research his Nick Cass identity.

Almost. But not quite.

Laura understood Nick's nervousness as his first encounter with AbaCo's lawyers loomed only a few hours away. But there was something else going on with him. He kept checking his cell phone like he was expecting a message, and the longer it didn't come, the more tense he was quietly becoming. It took knowing him exceedingly well to see the signs of his stress—the tightness around his eyes, the absent quality to some of his comments, the very occasional twitch of a thumb. She had to give Nick credit. He had amazing self-discipline to give away so little as a limousine whisked the two of them toward Washington, D.C.

His self-control held through the hearing, but he wasn't put on the witness stand and grilled, either. The legal proceeding mostly consisted of motions and technical arguments between the lawyers. As far as she could tell, they were wrangling over the rules of engagement for the trial to come. All in all, it was rather anticlimactic.

The hearing was adjourned, and Nick joined her in the aisle, looping an arm over her shoulder as they stepped outside…

…into a barrage of lights and microphones and shouted questions.

Nick reared back hard beside her, going board stiff. The Tatum team of attorneys leaped forward to intercept the phalanx of reporters, but it was too late. The press had spotted Nick. The story of his kidnapping and rescue had made a brief sensation last year, but thanks to his inability at the time to give interviews and put a poster-boy face to the story, it had faded quickly.

Unfortunately, the media had put two and two together, and they wanted the scoop on the miracle man now. Laura was half-blinded by flashing lights exploding at them from all directions. Good thing she was completely out of her old line of work. One media assault like this would've blown her cover permanently.

Nick swore quietly beside her. To the lawyers, he said tersely, "Get us out of here. Now."

The Tatum support team hustled her and Nick down the front steps and into the waiting limousine. He collapsed on the plush upholstery, swearing steadily under his breath in what sounded like Greek. What was up with that?

The car door closed, and silence descended around them.

He yanked out his cell phone and punched in a number. She caught only the first few digits—617 area code. Boston?

"It's Nick Cass," said into the device tersely. "What have you got for me?"

He listened in silence for a long time, his jaw clenching tighter with each passing minute. And then he finally ordered, "Keep looking."

"Who was that?" Laura asked as he put away his phone.

He looked up at her grimly. It was like staring into the eyes of a total stranger. Cold shock washed over her. Who was this man sitting beside her? She couldn't ever recall seeing that expression of irritation or determination in his gaze before.

He answered tightly, "That was my past."

She waited for him to elaborate but was immensely frustrated when he didn't. It was all she could do not to demand answers right this second. But she'd vowed when she found him to just be grateful that he was alive and accept whatever part of him he chose to share with her, no questions asked. But, darn, that was hard to stick to now!

The ride home was silent, with him lost in his thoughts, and her convincing herself to respecting his privacy. She would *not* turn her investigative skills on the father of her children, the man she loved with all her heart. She would trust him and take him at his word and support him. But her fingers literally itched to start typing, to dig into the internet and tap her network of resources built up over years of hunting down disappeared and deadbeat dads.

At dinner that night, she and Nick let Adam dominate the conversation with an eager description of his outing with Nanny Lisbet to Colonial Williamsburg that afternoon. Afterwards, Adam went upstairs with Lisbet to take a bath, and Laura and Nick adjourned to the family room. Nick flipped on the news.

Laura started violently as his face flashed up on the flat-screen TV at several times larger than life size. He froze on the sofa beside her.

The reporter narrated over footage from the courthouse this afternoon, recapping the story of Nick's rescue from a container ship a year before and moving on to report in detail how federal prosecutors were going after several high-ranking AbaCo executives for their roles in Nick's kidnapping. The reporter devolved into speculating on how high in the company the complicity reached.

Nick turned off the TV, scowling ferociously.

Laura commented soothingly, "It was an essentially accurate report. You came off completely sympathetically. You're an innocent victim of a heinous crime. And I have to say, you're incredibly photogenic. The public is going to love you." She smiled. "Particularly women."

His scowl deepened and he leaped up off the sofa to pace. He kept mumbling something under his breath that sounded like, "Not good. They'll see me."

"Who'll see you?" she asked carefully.

When he turned to stare at her, it was like looking into the eyes of a wild creature, hunted and cornered. "Everything will be ruined," he bit out. And with that, he stormed out of the room.

Laura eyed her laptop computer. Just a quick search. Nothing in depth. A brief check to see if something about his past would pop up. No, darn it! She headed for the gym in the basement to drown her temptation in some good old-fashioned sweat.

Nick was restless that night. To her vast disappointment, he didn't come to bed when she did, and the clock was turning toward 4:00 a.m. when he finally slipped in beside her. His arms went around her and she snuggled into his embrace, pretending to sleep.

But as she lay there in the dark, listening to his quiet breathing, she couldn't help but wonder who exactly she was in bed with. What in his past had him so frantic? Was he a criminal after all? Who were his enemies? What baggage clung to him? What kind of trouble was he so afraid of bringing to her doorstep? She was a former CIA field agent, for goodness' sake. What was so bad that he didn't think she could handle it?

She finally gave up on getting any more rest at around 6 a.m. and eased out of bed quietly so as not to wake Nick. She went to the nursery and scooped up Ellie who, orderly child that she was, was beginning to rouse exactly on time for her 6 a.m. feeding.

"Such a good baby," Laura crooned as she sat down in the rocking chair in the family room to feed Ellie. As the baby latched on and began sucking hungrily, Laura picked up the remote control and flipped on the TV. Was Nick still the star attraction of the all news channels, or had some real story come along overnight to bump him off the airwaves?

"...reclusive billionaire Nikolas Spiros may have surfaced yesterday in a Washington, D.C. courtroom...appears to be living under a new name...rumors of kidnapping and conspiracy surround his disappearance six years ago after a mental breakdown...unable to contact his people to confirm or deny his identity...you judge for yourself."

Laura lurched up out of the chair as a photograph of a dashing man in his early thirties was flashed up beside a still picture of Nick yesterday on the courthouse steps.

She knew that younger man very well, indeed. He'd been her lover in Paris six years ago. He was the father of her son. And the man in the other, more recent, picture was the man she lived with now, the father of her daughter. Ellie squawked as she lost her grip on breakfast, and Laura was momentarily distracted resettling the baby.

"I'm sorry, honey," she murmured. "Mommy was just surprised."

Although surprised hardly described the sick nausea rumbling through her gut. Nick was a Greek shipping tycoon named Nikolas Spiros? A billionaire? Why had he turned his back on all that? Why did he continue to live under this Nick Cass identity?

Her mind flashed back to Paris. To meeting Nick Cass there. *He'd lied to her.* He hadn't told her who he was back then, and he was perpetuating the lie now. No wonder neither she nor her attorney had been able to learn anything about him back then. Nick Cass didn't exist. The first stirrings of anger started low in her belly, building by steady degrees. Only Ellie's tiny body nestled against her breast, sucking sleepily, kept her from storming up the stairs and bursting in on Nick—Nikolas—this very second and demanding the full truth and nothing but the truth.

Who in the world was he?

Chapter 5

Laura reached her desk just as the phone rang. Who on earth would be calling her at this time of morning? Alarmed, she picked up the receiver.

"Good morning, this is Shelley Hacker from *The Morning News Hour*. I'm calling to speak to Nikolas Spiros."

"I'm afraid you have a wrong number." Laura hung up fast, not giving the reporter time to ask any follow-up questions.

The phone rang again. Oh, Lord. She glanced at the caller ID: *unknown caller.* She picked the receiver up an inch and set it back down. The feeding frenzy had begun.

"What's going on?"

Laura whirled to face Nick. "You tell me. The phone's ringing off the hook with reporters wanting to speak with Nikolas Spiros."

Beneath his olive complexion, Nick went a sickly shade of gray. He gritted out, "I'm Nick Cass."

"You are now. I get that. But were you this Spiros guy at some point in your past?"

"My past is dead."

She gritted her teeth. This was about her and the children as much as it was about him, darn it. She had a family to protect. "I understand your desire to move on. To start a new life. I really do. I support you all the way. But if you were Nikolas Spiros before, you're going to have to deal with him sometime. What are you going to tell the media?"

"I'll tell them nothing. It's none of their business."

A new hardness, or maybe an old hardness for all she knew, clung to Nick. This was not the gentle, laid-back man she'd spent the past year with. This man resembled much more a savvy, tough businessman who might run a billion-dollar shipping empire. Did she know him *at all*?

The phone rang again. She glanced at the caller ID and stopped herself at the last second from hanging it up. "It's Tatum Carter. Your lawyer wants to talk to you… Nikolas."

Nick sighed and held a hand out for the receiver.

"What the hell's going on, Nick?"

"Tatum. Good morning. I gather you've seen the news?" Nick asked evenly.

"What's this about you being some Greek billionaire? Hell, you owned AbaCo Shipping until a few years ago. What have you gotten me into?"

Ahh, the ass-covering had commenced. Nick sighed. "If you want to remove yourself from this case, I won't stop you."

"No, no," Tatum quickly replied. "I just want to know what's going on."

Nick rolled his eyes. Greed won out, then. He took a certain comfort in knowing what made the attorney tick. And then he jolted as he realized his old, sharklike business instincts were roaring back to the fore. He didn't want to return to this part of his life, this part of himself.

He glanced up and caught Laura staring at him in equal parts dismay and horror. He was losing her. As sure as he was standing here, she was pulling away from him—from the stranger he'd become. "I'll call you later, Tatum."

He hung up on the man without any further ado and sat down beside Laura on the sofa. "I lied to you in Paris."

"I already figured that out," she replied dryly. "Why?"

No way was he going to tell her all the things William Ward had revealed to him. There was still a chance he could keep her and the kids out of his past, and he was going to do his darnedest to make that happen. The private investigator had found nothing on any Nick Cass. So far it appeared such a man had never existed. If that held true, his new family was in the clear.

He shrugged. "I apparently created an alter ego for myself. An identity under which I could travel anonymously and unobtrusively. Nick Cass could go into a coffee shop or sit at a café and no one paid any attention to him."

"Who were you hiding from?" Laura asked shrewdly.

"The media, I imagine. My employees, maybe. Hell, maybe an ex-lover." He added candidly, "And myself, if I had to guess."

"Why didn't you tell me who you were?"

"I expect you fell for Nick Cass, the regular guy, not some Greek billionaire. Knowing you and loving you the way I do now, I'll bet I wasn't about to risk what I had with you."

"So you *lied* to me? You trusted me so

little? Didn't you think I would understand? Am I that judgmental or just that stupid?"

She didn't raise her voice, but the anger in it was unmistakable.

"I'm sorry, Laura. I don't remember any of it. I have no answers for you. Undoubtedly, I was wrong and should have told you every-thing from the start."

She threw up her hands. "Do you have any idea how hard it is to be this furious with you and not be able to be mad at you because you can't remember doing any of it?"

He smiled sadly. "I really am sorry."

"What are you going to do now?"

"Deal with the fallout as best as I can, and when the excitement blows over, go back to being plain old Nick Cass, the man who loves you and our kids."

"What fallout should I expect from this revelation?"

He grimaced but forced himself to look her squarely in the eye. "I honestly don't know. But I can tell you this. I plan to do everything in my power to keep you and the kids out of this."

"This *what?*"

She was too smart for her own good, sometimes. She'd heard the evasion in his voice and put her finger exactly on the source of his discomfort. "I've had a gut feeling since the moment you fished me out of that box that I should let sleeping dogs lie. I feel that way more strongly than ever. It's nothing concrete. Just a feeling."

He reached out and took her icy hands in his. "I don't know what's hidden in those lost five years, I swear. But I think it's bad, and I think it could put you and the children in danger. You've got to let me deal with this alone. Stay away from it, Laura."

She stared at him, her dark gaze brimming with frustration. "No way—"

He cut her off gently. "I have to know the children are safe. You have to take care of them for me—for us—while I put my past to rest."

Ellie must've sensed her mother's tension for the infant started to fuss. He was a cad to be so relieved at being saved by a baby's distress. Ellie, uncharacteristically, wanted no part of being soothed. Her fussing escalated to crying outright and soon to screaming. Not appreciating mommy's stress, apparently.

Laura spared him a look that promised this conversation was not over as she left to find Lisbet.

The phone rang again. He glanced at the caller ID and jolted. William Ward. How had his former attorney found this phone number, and furthermore, why on earth was he calling it? Nick picked up the receiver quickly lest Laura take the call.

"Good morning, William."

"Nikolas. We need to talk."

"Then speak."

"This is confidential. Needs to be face-to-face."

Nick sighed. "In case you haven't seen the

news this morning, I'm a little busy at the moment." Not to mention he had serious damage control to do with Laura. He knew her well enough to know that she wasn't about to let him deal with this mess on his own.

The lawyer huffed and then said heavily, "I've been doing some digging about you. I've found something. It's bad."

Nick froze. "What is it?"

"I'm at my beach house on the Cape. Get here as fast as you can."

"I can't just drop everything here and come see you!" Nick exploded. "The AbaCo trial is about to begin. And furthermore, my old life is *over*. Finished. I'm not that person anymore."

"Based on what's sitting on my desk in front of me, your old life is about to come after you whether you like it or not."

"I won't let my past *touch* my new life," Nick bit out sharply. He turned to pace and stopped in his tracks. Laura. She was standing in the doorway, the color draining from her face as he watched.

"I've got to go," Nick snapped.

William said forcefully, "I'm not kidding. You need to come up here—"

He hung up on the lawyer.

"What's up?" Laura asked. Her cool voice sounded brittle, like she was barely hanging on to self-control.

"My past," he bit out. "I don't know." He shoved a frustrated hand through his hair. "I don't remember any of it."

"You knew your real name. It would've taken you two minutes on the internet to find out all about yourself, and maybe even what's got you all freaked out."

How was he supposed to explain his dead certainty that he had to leave his past alone? To stay far, far away from anything having to do with Nikolas Spiros? It would sound like a lame excuse to her. Hell, maybe it was a lame excuse.

Laura's voice fell, dropping into a hurt hush

that was a hundred times more painful than if she'd yelled at him. "I thought you loved me."

He didn't try to stop her as she whirled and ran from the room. He'd been worse than a fool to avoid his past, and she was right to be furious with him. Every accusation she'd thrown at him was less awful than the ones he was flinging at himself right now. It didn't even make things better that he was dying inside. She was everything to him, and he'd hurt her terribly. He'd rather endure torture than cause her an ounce of pain. But he'd pretty well blown that. He'd blown *everything*.

Now what was he supposed to do? How was he ever going to make this better?

Swearing long and hard at himself, he headed upstairs to Adam's room. The child was still asleep, which was just as well. He didn't think he'd have the strength to say goodbye to his son if Adam were awake. Stroking the dark, silky hair so like his own gently, he murmured, "I love you more than life. Never doubt that. Take care of your mother for me. And be brave."

He turned and left quickly before he could weaken. He had to protect them all. No matter the cost to himself. Feeling every bit of the past six years in his bones, an ache that had never quite gone away, he headed downstairs. Laura and the kids had kept it at bay with their love and laughter, but all of a sudden, the withheld agony was back.

"Are you going out, Mr. Cass?" Marta asked in surprise. "Breakfast will be ready soon."

He rasped, "I won't be taking breakfast today. And you'd better send Laura's up to her office. I suspect she's going to be busy in there for a while."

By noon, with her connections she'd probably know more about Nick Cass than he did. And she would definitely know everything there was to know about Nikolas Spiros. Every last ugly, selfish, tawdry detail.

He'd lost her. The lies had finally caught up with him. *But, Lord, the cost of it.* His eyes hot and his throat painfully tight, he stepped out of the house and drove away from the best things that had ever happened to him. He'd ruined it all. Everything that was good and right about his life retreated in the rear-view mirror as he pulled out of the estate. If it was the last thing he ever did, he'd make this mess right. Put his family back together.

He thought he'd known hell before in a box. Hah! That had been a walk in a park compared to the hell embracing him now. A hell of his own making.

Laura was hanging on by a thread. The phone wouldn't quit ringing, and she was developing a horrendous headache. How on earth had she never connected Nick to Nikolas Spiros? She should have recognized him in Paris, and sometime in the past year she definitely should have searched for disappearances of men matching Nick's description six years ago. But no. He hadn't wanted to know, and she'd gone along with his plan to bury their heads in the sand and avoid facing whatever demons lurked in his past. She'd willfully ignored the signs that Nick was not what he appeared to be, had been so caught up in her own selfish bliss that she hadn't asked any of the obvious questions.

Why didn't he have any other family or friends he wanted to let know he was alive and free? Why was he so at ease living in the luxurious world she inhabited? Why did he flatly refuse to talk about his past prior to his memory loss? And the granddaddy of them all—why was he kidnapped and thrown into a box for five years? Who were his enemies, and why did they bear him so much malice that they chose to make him suffer rather than simply kill him?

At lunchtime, Lisbet apologetically poked her head into Laura's office. "I'm sorry, ma'am, but Adam is hysterical and really needs to be with you. I've tried everything

I know to calm him, but he's panicked that something bad has happened to you and his father. Nothing will do but for him to see you."

Laura stood up quickly. The needs of her children would always come first over her work...even if that work was investigating their father. She hurried to the playroom, where Adam was curled up in a sobbing ball in the corner, hugging the stuffed elephant that had been his special toy forever.

Laura stroked his back gently. "Hey, kiddo. What's the matter?"

The child flung himself at her, wrapping his arms around her neck and squeezing her tightly enough that it was a little hard to breathe. Not that she complained. She hugged his shaking body. "Everything's okay," she soothed him, rocking back and forth.

"Daddy's gone, and the bad man got him!"

"Daddy's not gone. And the bad man definitely didn't get him," Laura declared.

Lisbet cleared her throat. "Begging your

pardon, but Mr. Cass left the house before breakfast."

Laura's entire being clenched in shock. He'd left? Where had he gone? And for how long? She shoved back her panic, focusing for the moment on her son. "Adam, Daddy has some business to take care of. It's all right."

"No, it's not. He told me to take care of you for him. And to be brave. He wouldn't say that if he was coming back. He went to fight the bad man."

"Well, honey, even if he did, Daddy will win. It'll be okay."

"No, it won't!" Adam wailed.

"Do you need me to go help Daddy?"

Adam lifted his red, wet gaze to hers. "Can you do that?"

"Sure. I'm pretty ferocious, you know."

"Daddy says you're like a mama bear with cubs," Adam replied dryly, his humor already so much like his father's.

A burning knife twisted in her gut. She replied stoutly, "He's right. Grrrr."

Adam smiled reluctantly. But he wasn't about to be diverted so easily. "You won't let the bad man get you, too?"

"Never."

"Promise?"

"I promise. Cross my heart, hope to die, alligator in my eye."

"Alligator in your—" Adam giggled. "That's silly."

"Made you laugh, didn't it?"

"Yes." He waxed thoughtful once more. Impossible to distract, he was. Just like both of his parents on that score. "Where do you think the bad man is?"

"Hmm. I don't know. But I'm really, really good at finding people. I found Daddy before, didn't I? I'll find the bad man, and I'll find Daddy, again. I'd never let anything happen to anyone in our family. I'm a mama bear, and you and Ellie are my cubs. Don't you ever forget that, okay?"

Adam nodded against her neck.

She closed her eyes and prayed for strength. She had to find Nick. Figure out what had gone so wrong so fast. And somehow, some way, put it right. Her children needed their father.

Chapter 6

Laura was startled when Marta announced that Tatum Carter was at the house and waiting in the library to speak with her. Since when did lawyers make house calls? He must be panicked over Nick's abrupt disappearance yesterday. *Join the club.*

She left her computer, which had been giving up a treasure trove of information on one Nikolas Spiros, and walked down the hall to the library. "Tatum. This is a pleasant surprise. What can I do for you today?"

"Tell me where Nick is. The feds are going to have my head on a platter if I lose their star witness for them. The trial starts next week."

She replied quietly, "If I knew where he was, do you think I'd be standing here talking to you?"

"What the hell's going on with him, Laura?"

She sighed. "I think we all underestimated the trauma he's suffering from. And I think we all ignored the possible problems his memory loss could be concealing."

"What's your gut feel about him? Is he stable enough to put on a witness stand? If AbaCo skates on this kidnapping charge, it'll be like letting Al Capone get off on the tax evasion charges that finally landed him in jail where he belonged."

She wasn't concerned about Nick's stability as much as she was about the state of his heart. Had he already abandoned her and the kids and returned to his old life? Goodness knew, Nikolas Spiros had lived a life of glamorous excess that went well beyond even her wealth to provide.

She spoke with a conviction she was far from feeling. "If Nick goes on the witness stand, he'll do what he has to do to put away his captors." *Even if it messes up his personal life? Costs him the Spiros fortune?* She'd like to think he was that honorable, but at this point, she had no way of knowing.

"Where is he, Laura? What's your best guess?"

"My best guess—" her best hope "—is that he's gone away to deal with the fallout of his past and that he'll be back when it's resolved."

"How long is that going to take? He's got about a week to get his ducks in line."

She shrugged. If only Nick had confided in her. Had let her help him. She had enormous resources, official and unofficial, at her fingertips with which to help him. She understood his impulse to protect her and the kids, to keep his new life far away from his old one. But she was still as frustrated as all get out at her current helplessness. If only she knew where he was!

"Tatum, if you were a wealthy man who's

been out of touch with his life for a while, where would you go to pick up the threads?"

"Easy. My stock broker and my lawyer."

She nodded. "How do I go about finding out who Nick's—Nikolas's—personal attorney was six years ago?"

Tatum frowned. "Client lists are confidential. But I could make a few phone calls. Maybe find out something off the record. Where was Nick living prior to his kidnapping?"

"His shipping empire was headquartered in Athens and had offices all around the world." *Including Paris.* "His North American headquarters was in Boston."

Tatum called an attorney buddy of his from law school who practiced in Boston. That guy didn't know anything, but referred Tatum to someone else. As the lawyer placed a second call, she reflected on the enormous power of good-old-boy networks.

The second lawyer knew something. She

could tell by the way Tatum's face lit up as he listened intently.

"Ward, MacIntosh and Howe," Tatum announced as he disconnected the call. "Want me to contact them and see if Nick's been in their offices recently?"

"Sure."

If Nick had been to visit his lawyer, he might still be in the Boston area. During his incarceration, his shipping company had been sold out from under him, and he might very well be trying to reverse that sale. If not that, Nick was probably getting funds released into his hands to finance whatever he planned to do next. She had an alert set on their joint bank accounts to notify her the second Nick accessed any of them, but so far, he hadn't. He was welcome to whatever he needed or wanted from her accounts.

Funny how love and family made something like money seem so trivial. Not that she'd ever been that hung up on wealth. She just wanted to have enough to do what she wanted to without having to worry about it. Case in point: It had been handy over the past five years to finance her own investigations as she helped women find the fathers of their children. Most of her clients had been in desperate financial straits and couldn't have paid her a dime even if they'd known who she was.

Tatum was on hold with Nick's law firm and muttering to himself as he waited. "…fly up to Boston and try to contact him before the federal prosecutors get wind of the fact that he's fled."

"I don't think he's fled," she responded. "I think he's taking care of personal business."

"Yeah, well, he'd better take care of it fast—" He broke off and spoke into the phone. "This is Tatum Carter of Carter and Associates in Fairfax, Virginia. I represent Nick Cass—Nikolas Spiros—in an upcoming trial against the people who allegedly kidnapped him. I need to speak with Nick's attorney at your firm."

Laura frowned as Carter visibly paled.

"I'm so sorry," he stammered. "I'll be in touch in a few days. Of course. My sympathies."

Alarmed, Laura blurted the second he hung up, "What happened? What's wrong?"

"Nick's lawyer is dead. Someone broke into the guy's house last night. The police think William Ward startled the intruder and was murdered."

Warning bells clanged wildly in Laura's head. Home robbery, her foot. What were the odds that someone randomly broke into the lawyer's house the day after his kidnapped billionaire client surfaced? *Ohmigosh. Nick.* How much danger was he in? Her gut yelled that he was the prime target on the hit list.

"I have to go, Carter. I'll be in touch." She raced out of the room and upstairs to pack. Somewhere in the next ten frantic minutes, she ordered up an emergency corporate jet to fly her to Boston ASAP.

Ellie squawked over the baby monitor,

startling Laura out of her panicked packing. The baby. What was she going to do about her daughter? The infant nursed exclusively, and after her recent bout of jaundice, Laura was loathe to shift Ellie over to formula. She didn't have enough pumped milk in the freezer to be gone for several days.

Laura closed her eyes in frustration. Mother or frantic lover? How was she supposed to choose between the two? With a sigh, she headed for the nursery to feed the baby. Afterward, she quickly packed a bag for Ellie as well.

She popped into the playroom to say goodbye to Adam. "Hey, kiddo."

He flung himself at her and she laughed as he planted a sticky kiss on her cheek. "I'm off to go rescue Daddy. Call me whenever you want to, okay?"

Adam nodded against her neck. "Promise you'll save Daddy from the bad man."

"You've got it. I promise. Daddy and I will be home in no time. You and Lisbet have fun while I'm gone and don't eat anything healthy, okay?"

Adam laughed. They both knew his health-freak nanny would never dream of letting Adam exist on junk food.

"I love you, Adam."

"Love you, too, Mommy."

Her heart ached at having to leave her precious son for even a few days. She nodded at Lisbet over Adam's dark head, and the nanny smiled and nodded back. Lisbet knew full well how deeply Laura treasured her children and would take care of Adam like her own son in Laura's absence.

"I'll be back as soon as I can. No more than, say, three days."

"Yes, ma'am. Have a safe trip."

Before she could dissolve into completely un-superhero-like tears in front of her son, Laura spun and left the playroom, giving a theatric leap as she passed through the doorway. "Super Mommy away!" she called out.

The last sound she heard as she scooped

up Ellie and headed out was Adam shouting, "Go, Super Mommy!"

The drive to the airport and subsequent flight to Boston took several hours. It was late afternoon when Laura and Ellie arrived at Logan Airport. The baby traveled like a champ. She must take after her mother when it came to enjoying adventure and new experiences.

A newspaper purchased in the airport terminal told Laura that William Ward had been at his home on Cape Cod when he was killed. She plugged the town into her rental car's GPS and in a few minutes was crawling down I-93 in the remnants of the day's rush-hour traffic. Big Dig or no Big Dig, traffic in Boston was horrendous.

It was nearly 10:00 p.m. when she finally found Ward's house just outside Hyannis-port. In full spy mode, she turned off her headlights and drove past. It was impossible to miss with yellow crime scene tape stretched all around it. She turned down the first side road and parked parallel to Ward's house. Time to go cross-country. Although how Super Mommy was supposed to pull that off with a baby in tow, she wasn't sure.

She donned a baby backpack and settled Ellie into a nest of blankets within it. The baby had just dined and was ready for a nice warm nap. Thankfully, as Laura set out hiking toward the Ward house, the motion seemed to soothe her daughter.

Ward was not a criminal lawyer, which eliminated some disgruntled client or victim of one of his clients being the killer. It had to be Nick who triggered the attack. What information could Ward have on Nikolas Spiros that was worth killing for? Laura had no idea what it could be, but she'd bet Nick had a good idea what it was. Or if Nick didn't know what it was, he'd darn well be dying of curiosity to know. And in either case, she figured Nick planned to find out what information Ward had been murdered over.

A clearing came into sight ahead. Assuming she hadn't lost all of her CIA field skills, that would be the backyard of the Ward house. Hopefully, Nick would be paying this place a visit soon. And if she was lucky, she just might spot him and hook up with him. At least that was the plan. It was admittedly a sketchy plan, but better than having no plan at all. Given that Nick hadn't used any of his credit cards and still had not withdrawn any funds from their checking accounts, she could only assume he was using cash and an assumed name. It was what she'd do in the same situation. And Nick was nothing if not highly intelligent.

She cursed under her breath as a branch whapped her in the face, showering her with wet, cold dew. She hadn't snuck around in the woods for years, and she abruptly remembered why she'd never liked this sort of work. She'd always been more at ease in urban environments and had gravitated to assignments in major metropolitan areas. Like Paris.

Ellie made an unhappy noise as some of the cold dew sprinkled her. Laura reached awkwardly to pat her. "Hush, sweetie. Mommy's trying to be sneaky."

Although how on God's green earth she was going to pull that off with an infant in tow, she had no idea. It was pure insanity to try it. But for now, Ellie was stuck in the woods playing spy with Mommy.

Laura pushed forward a few more yards and the baby bag caught on a bush. Of course, it spilled. Swearing under her breath, she crouched and picked up miscellaneous baby gear and stuffed it all back in the bag.

She rose to her feet and continued forward.

If William Ward's killers had broken into his house to kill him instead of in a simple mugging or drive-by shooting, that meant his killers also had orders to search for something. Something in this house.

She stopped in the shadow of a huge tree as

Ward's "cottage" came into view. The house had to have at least five bedrooms, if not more. If that was a cottage, then it was a cottage on serious steroids. The sound and smell of the ocean were unmistakable as Laura reached the edge of the woods crowding the rear of the structure. No wonder the killers had gotten away last night. This forest made for a perfect escape route.

She hunkered down to wait for someone to show up and prayed it would be Nick and not the killers coming back to finish their search. Time passed, and Ellie snoozed happily at her back. The baby was like having her own personal heater snuggled up against her. Laura's legs got stiff, and she moved through the trees until she could see the front of the house. The front porch was brick with tall white pillars and looked strangely out of place on the otherwise Craftsman-style home.

"How tacky," she muttered to Ellie.

Ellie stirred long enough to burble her

disapproval of the architectural faux pas as headlights came into view on the road in front of the house. Laura plastered herself against a tree trunk as a sedan pulled up in front of the house. A tall form unfolded from the driver's seat and Laura gasped in spite of herself. He might be wearing a gray wig and be hunching over as if he were decades older, but there was no mistaking Nick.

His head came up sharply, almost as if he'd heard her. But surely that wasn't possible over the roar of the ocean behind him. She didn't put it past him to sense her presence, however. In her experience, people often became incredibly intuitive in high-threat situations. And there was no denying that the connection between them had always been electric.

She watched tensely as Nick approached the house. He had the good sense to walk around the house and approach it from the back, out of sight of the road. She drifted along beside him, maintaining her cover in the trees. How was he going to get in? As far as she knew, he had no particular skills in breaking and entering. She was startled when he merely stepped up to the alarm pad by the back door and entered a series of numbers. He reached for the back door and slipped inside.

Her spy within was indignant at how easily he'd gained entrance. She'd have been forced to go through a lengthy and difficult process to bypass the security system and pick the door lock. But the woman within who worried about Nick was incredibly relieved that he was safely inside.

She was just stepping clear of the woods when a quiet sound in the dark threw Laura onto full battle alert. It was a car. Coming down the road with its headlights off. Nobody with honest intentions drove around on a cloudy night on an isolated road like this with no lights. Crud. She had to let Nick know he was about to have company. She eyed the open expanse of lawn between her and the house warily.

If she was going to go, it had to be right now before the darkened car turned into the drive. She took off running as fast as she could. God bless her personal trainer for the misery he'd put her through this past month. She wasn't in the best shape of her entire life, but at least she wasn't a complete marshmallow.

She darted onto the back porch as Ellie roused, complaining about being jostled around so hard in the baby carrier.

"It's okay, sweetie. Go back to sleep," Laura soothed as she pushed open the already partially ajar door. She closed it behind her and somewhere nearby, the house's security system beeped, reactivating.

She slipped into the deep shadows of a coat room and then into a kitchen. She had to hurry. The bad guys would be here in a minute or so. "Nick!" she called out. She moved into a long hallway that led toward the front of the house. "Nick!"

He emerged from what looked like an office, looking thunderstruck. "Laura? What are you doing here?"

"Later," she bit out. "We're about to have company. The kind with guns."

Nick darted to a window to look outside. "I don't see anyone."

"They've pulled around back, then. Can we open the front door without setting off the alarm system?" she asked urgently.

"Who cares? Let's set it off. The police will be here in a few minutes and it'll chase off these bastards in the meantime."

She nodded and they stepped forward. That was when he spotted Ellie.

"You brought the baby with you?" he exclaimed incredulously.

"I'm a nursing mother, and I wasn't exactly expecting armed men to threaten us," she snapped. "Let's go. They'll be inside any second."

Nick nodded.

She nodded back and he opened the front door. A piercing alarm screeched deafeningly as they raced across the front porch. Ellie lurched against Laura's back and immediately commenced screaming at the top of her lungs. It was that special, baby-in-mortal-danger wail that absolutely demanded an instant response, and it was all Laura could do to keep running across the front yard toward Nick's car and not stop to comfort her.

A bang behind her and a simultaneous metallic ping in front of her did get an immediate reaction out of Laura, however. Someone was *shooting* at them! Ducking instinctively, she looked over her shoulder. A dark figure was coming around the corner of the house.

Out of her peripheral vision, she caught sight of a second figure coming around the other side of the house. Plus a third man entering the house…she swore mentally. She and Nick were outnumbered, which meant they were also outgunned.

The two men advanced cautiously, not shooting any more after that first volley of shots aimed at Nick's car. Then it hit her. The shooters must have disabled the vehicle so she and Nick couldn't escape. *Which meant they wanted to capture Nick.*

No! Not again! He couldn't disappear again. This time it would undoubtedly be for good. They'd capture him over her dead body. Super Mommy roared to the fore, and Laura fumbled frantically in the baby bag banging around at her side as she ran after Nick.

"Your car's dead," she panted. "Mine's that way."

He veered in the direction she pointed and sprinted for the woods with her on his heels.

Her fingers frantically identified objects inside the baby bag. Bottle. Diaper ointment. Pacifier. Dammit, where was her gun? Finally, she felt its cold weight and yanked it clear of the fabric bag. She and Nick gained the edge of the woods and slowed down to navigate the heavy underbrush. Thankfully, Ellie had fallen mostly silent. Nick held back a jumble of vines for her and she slipped past him. She turned to face their pursuers. The pair of men were advancing slowly, now, weapons held out in front of them in grips that looked entirely too competent for Laura's comfort.

"My car's through the woods," she whispered urgently. "That way."

Nick whispered back, "You go first. I'll go behind you. That way if they shoot at us they'll hit me and not Ellie."

"Take my pistol."

He reached under his coat. "I have one. Keep yours."

Where in the heck had he gotten a hold of a gun? Did he even know how to use the thing? She eyed him in dismay but was relieved to see him holding it in a reasonable grip. They might just get out of this alive, after all. If they could keep Ellie quiet so she wouldn't give their position away.

Nick moved close as they crept forward cautiously. He crooned to Ellie, "Hush, sweetheart. Be an angel for Daddy."

How he could be so cool with armed men chasing them, she had no idea. Shockingly, his calm tone seemed to mollify the baby and she quieted completely.

"That's my brave girl," Nick continued to murmur.

Laura looked back over her shoulder. The pair of men had been joined by a third and they were moving cautiously in this direction. She and Nick needed a diversion. Something dramatic. She dug around in the baby bag until she felt the steel cylinder of a silencer. She screwed it onto her weapon, assumed a shooter's stance, took careful aim and fired at the gaudy chandelier on the front porch. It exploded spectacularly, glass shattering in all directions, and the three men ducked at the abrupt noise behind them.

Laura sprinted like a madwoman through the woods with Nick panting right on her heels as they dodged left and right around trees. Shots rang out behind them. Thankfully, in the real world, most people couldn't hit the broad side of the barn when they were running themselves and aiming at another fast-moving target.

Bark flew nearby. Uh-oh. It didn't look like their pursuers were shooting to take out tires anymore. That looked like a shot aimed to kill.

Waaaaaah! Ellie let out a renewed scream.

Laura fumbled through the contents of the bag desperately, as she ran, seeking the familiar shape of the pacifier. Ammo clip. Bottle. Diapers. No pacifier!

Bingo. A soft rubber nipple. Laura yanked it out as she ducked under a low branch. She stumbled as her foot slid off a half-rotted log buried in the leaves, staggered left and barely managed to right herself. But she'd dropped the all-important pacifier. She paused a precious second to look around. Thank God.

White plastic caught her eye. Laura pounced on it and took off running once more.

The men behind them were close enough for her to hear their heavy breathing. At this range, they might actually hit a moving target. She put on a terrified burst of speed, zigzagging like a rabbit fleeing for its life.

Ellie's screaming took on a rhythmic quality as the baby was jostled by Laura's steps. No way were they going to escape their pursuers until the child quit giving away their position like this. They needed to turn this into a stealth exercise.

More gunshots rang out behind them. Nick swore behind Laura. "Hurry," he grunted. "That was close."

Desperate, she wiped the pacifier on her shirt and stabbed backward over her shoulder. She was so going to mommy hell already for putting her child in the line of fire, she supposed giving her a dirty pacifier wouldn't make matters much worse. But what choice did she have? It was that or die.

Miraculously, she hit Ellie's mouth, and even more miraculously, the infant took the pacifier, sucking it angrily. Laura slowed, ducking into an area of thick brush. Nick followed closely, helping her lift brambles aside as they crept forward. Male voices called back and forth behind them. Apparently, their pursuers had lost sight of them. Hallelujah.

She pointed off to their left in the direction she thought the car was, assuming she wasn't completely disoriented out here in the pitch-black night and bewildering tangle of trees and undergrowth, and Nick veered that direction.

They burst out of the trees as a dirt road opened up before them. "This way," she gasped. The car's blessed bulk came into sight and she nearly sobbed in relief. Nick hung back a little, still protecting Ellie with his body as Laura used the last of her strength to tear toward the vehicle.

"I'll drive," Nick called out low behind her.

Like any good field operative, she'd left the doors unlocked and the key fob inside the vehicle. She dived for the passenger door and flung herself inside awkwardly, half-lying across the front seat so she wouldn't crush Ellie, while Nick leaped into the driver's seat and punched the ignition button. He wasted no time throwing the vehicle into gear and stomping on the gas. The car jumped forward.

Shots behind them announced that the bad guys had reached the road. The car squealed around a curve and the shooting behind them stopped.

"They'll follow us," Nick announced.

"Then drive like a bat out of hell," she panted back.

While he commenced doing just that, she wriggled out of the backpack and half-climbed over the backseat to strap Ellie, red-faced and furious, into her car seat. Laura wiped the pacifier off as best she could, and offered it to the baby once more.

Yup. Mommy hell for her. But sometimes a mommy had to do what a mommy had to do. And given that they were careening along a twisting dirt road at something like seventy miles per hour, she wasn't about to unstrap the infant and try to nurse her.

Nick muttered, white knuckled, "Mother of God, Laura, what are you doing here with Ellie?"

"Saving your life, apparently. Where did you learn to drive like this?"

"I'm told I did some Formula One racing in my previous life."

"Had a death wish, did you?"

"Something like that."

"Have you got more ammunition?" he asked.

Right. Because every prepared mommy hauled around extra ammunition along with spare diapers and a change of clothes for baby. She dug into the bottom of the baby bag for spare clips. She came up with two full fourteen-shot clips and counted back fast to the firefight in her head. "I've got nine shots in my weapon now and twenty-eight more here."

He nodded tersely. "I've got five shots left. I don't have spare clips. It was all I could do to buy an unregistered gun without getting arrested, let alone acquiring extra clips for it."

Ellie was finally subsiding. Laura smiled at the vigorous sucking noises coming from the car seat. It was good to know her daughter had spunk when provoked.

"Where does this road go?" Nick asked.

"I have no idea. There's not a straight road on the entire Cape. My suggestion is we keep driving until we get to some road the GPS recognizes."

He nodded tersely. "How did you find me?"

"Carter Tatum found out William Ward was your attorney. When we discovered he'd been killed, I figured it couldn't be a coincidence. Clearly, he had something the people out to get you want. Which meant you were bound to come looking for it, too. So, I staked out Ward's house and waited for you to show up."

"You know me too well."

She shrugged. "Lucky guess."

Nick smiled wryly. "Luck had nothing to do with it. I always knew you were brilliant."

"Are you going to let me use that brilliance to help you, now?"

He sighed. "I wanted to keep you out of this. I knew it could get dangerous, and I didn't want you or the kids to get hurt."

She winced at the faint note of reproach in his voice. He was right. She'd been an idiot to put Ellie in danger. But she'd only expected a nice, quiet stake-out. As soon as they were safe, she'd make other arrangements for the baby.

"I appreciate the sentiment, Nick, but it's time to let me help you. I'm good at this sort of thing, and I want my children's father alive." She carefully avoided adding that she wanted her lover alive, too. She had no idea whether or not he planned to remain with her now that his true identity was out in the open.

The dirt road abruptly intersected a paved road. Nick turned west and in a moment the GPS popped up a road map. They followed the residential street for a mile or so and turned onto a larger road. As Nick accelerated into the desultory traffic, she watched carefully in the rearview mirror for any sign of followers. No lights or cars were hanging behind them acting like tails.

They'd made it.

Her hands started to shake, and then her whole body got into the act. Nick glanced over at her in concern. "Are you okay?" he asked.

"No, I'm *not* okay. Would you care to tell me why those men just tried to kidnap you again?"

Nick frowned. "It looked to me like they were trying to kill us."

She shook her head in the negative. "They

didn't shoot at you when you were running across the lawn. They only fired at your car. They didn't want you to leave, but they didn't want you dead. In the woods, only a few of the shots came anywhere near us, and I think those were mistakes. They were trying to scare us into surrendering but definitely weren't trying to kill you. Which means someone wants you alive. I can only infer that means someone wants something from you."

Her declaration put a heavy frown on Nick's handsome features.

She continued, "Why weren't you killed six years ago? Why the elaborate kidnapping instead? I'll bet that's the same reason those men weren't trying to kill you tonight." Lord, it felt good to finally ask the question. "What's going *on,* Nick?"

Chapter 7

Nick sighed. Laura, of all people, deserved answers. Answers he was far from having, however. "I truly don't remember anything of those five years. I swear," he stated.

Laura nodded and crossed her arms expectantly, announcing silently that she wasn't going to back off this time. Her child had just been put in mortal danger, and she was at the end of her prodigious patience. Not that he blamed her. He just hoped she'd forgive him when she heard the entire, sordid tale. Although, it wasn't like he forgave himself.

He picked up the story reluctantly. "That trip I took a few days ago was to Boston to pay a visit to my old attorney, William Ward. It turned out he was able to fill in some pertinent details of the two years prior to my kidnapping."

When Laura opened her mouth to ask about it, he raised a hand gently for her to let him continue. She nodded and subsided.

"I'll fill you in on that in a minute. The morning after my face got splashed all over the news, William called me. He said he had important information to show me. He insisted I come up to his house on the Cape immediately."

"What was it?" Laura blurted.

"I don't know."

Her hopeful expression fell.

"But when we get somewhere safe, I have a flash drive in my pocket that I took from the secret drawer in William's desk. I'm hoping it'll give us some answers."

"How did you know about his house's security code, not to mention this secret drawer?"

He made a face. "William was practically

a second father to me. I spent a lot of time with him and his wife on the cape. He represented me when I turned eighteen and took over Spiros Shipping. He's been my attorney ever since."

"Who do you think killed him?"

"I have no idea."

Laura mulled things over, and Nick let her. In his experience, she was eminently reasonable when left to her own devices to figure a thing out. He only prayed that reason led her to accept his words as truth.

They were off the Cape and approaching Boston proper before she finally asked soberly, "Why do you think someone killed your lawyer?"

"I can think of about a billion reasons," he answered grimly.

She nodded in agreement. "I've been reading on the internet about the sale of Spiros Shipping after you dropped out of sight. I'm assuming someone faked your permission and sold it out from under you?"

"I don't know if they coerced me into signing something or just forged my signature. I can't imagine ever giving anyone permission to sell the family business."

"Who hated you enough to steal your business?"

He briefly considered pulling off the road to address her question but decided she'd be less likely to attack him if he were at the wheel of a moving car with her and Ellie in it. He answered carefully, "When you arrived at William Ward's house, I was browsing through the most recent documents on his computer."

"And?" she prompted cautiously.

"And it turns out that shortly before I met you in Paris, I took a secret trip to Las Vegas." Laura went still. She must see it coming. He continued grimly, "I wasn't alone on that trip. It turns out I was secretly married there to a woman named Meredith Black." The name felt strange on his tongue.

Vaguely unpleasant, like the remembered taste of bitter medicine.

If Laura had been still before, she went statuelike now. Alarmed, he alternated between glancing over at her and keeping an eye on the highway.

Finally, he couldn't stand the suspense of her complete nonreaction any longer. "Talk to me," he urged.

"What do you want me to say?" Laura's voice was hollow. Hoarse. Unlike how he'd ever heard it before. Guilt and self-loathing consumed him. He'd caused the woman he loved this pain.

He spoke in a rush. "I swear. I have no recollection of her whatsoever. I don't know why I married her, and I surely don't know why I got involved with you in Paris so soon afterward. I can only assume the marriage was an impulsive thing and didn't work out. Maybe I was drunk and it was all a big joke."

"A joke?" Laura choked out.

"A really, really bad one?" he offered.

Based on the thunderous frown settling on her brow, Laura clearly failed to see the humor. He didn't blame her.

He drove in silence while guilt and misery ate at his gut from the inside out. It was his worst nightmare come true. Something—someone—out of his past had the power to destroy everything he and Laura had built between them, including their happy little family. He'd contact this Meredith Black woman and get a divorce. The woman could have whatever financial resources had been left to Nikolas Spiros. He'd make it all better.

But then Laura asked, "Why hasn't she come forward or contacted you now that your face is being splashed all over the news?"

"Maybe she hasn't heard about me."

Laura snorted. "You're an international sensation. The playboy billionaire back from a mysterious, six-year absence. She'd have to be living in a cave not to have heard about you."

He frowned. Laura was right. Why hadn't

this Meredith person contacted him? Or had she? Was she the urgent reason William Ward had insisted on him coming to the Cape to discuss?

"Did she have control of your financial assets while you were gone?" Laura asked.

"I don't know. Possibly."

"Then your return would throw a serious monkey wrench into her life. You'd be a massive problem for her."

He laughed with scant humor. "Gee. Thanks."

"Sorry. Just trying to think like my enemy."

Warmth burst in his gut. If Laura considered Meredith her enemy, he almost felt sorry for the woman. But not quite.

Laura made an angry sound under her breath. He'd bet she wasn't even aware of having made it. Her unconscious loyalty warmed him all the way down to his soul.

"You truly have no recollection of her whatsoever?"

"None."

"Convenient," Laura muttered.

Alarmed, he glanced over at her. "I'm telling you the truth. I have no idea why I married her."

"She must be hell on wheels in the sack," Laura commented sourly.

Nick laughed. "I'll take you any day of the week and twice on Sunday over any other woman on the planet in that department."

Laura threw him a vaguely skeptical look. "The thirty-year-old mother of two with a body under attack by gravity and who needs a slave driver of a personal trainer to keep her even remotely non-jiggly these days?"

"Yes. Exactly," he replied firmly.

She didn't look convinced.

He swore mentally. Just how much damage control did he have ahead of him to convince Laura that, in spite of this wife, *she* was the love of his life?

"Could your wife be behind tonight's kidnapping attempt?"

The idea shocked him into silence.

Laura continued, "But why?"

"She wants to renew our vows?" he quipped.

"Not funny," Laura retorted.

He sighed. "I imagine she wants to aggressively renegotiate control of my estate."

"With a gun pointed at your head?"

"Precisely."

"Bitch," Laura breathed under her breath.

Nick laughed quietly. "My sentiments exactly."

"What are you going to do?"

"Give her whatever she wants to divorce me."

"She has probably taken almost everything you own already."

He shrugged. "I'm not concerned about the money. I can always make more. I just want to get away with my life and my soul intact. I refuse to live always looking over my shoulder, worried that she might come after you and the kids someday."

Laura's expression snapped closed. Unreadable. Stubborn enough to give him a severe and unpleasant jolt. "Are we okay?" he blurted.

"No, Nick. We're not okay. You're married to another woman. You knew who you were and didn't tell me. And now your past has put not only you, but me and Ellie, in danger."

He nodded slowly. He couldn't blame her for feeling any of that. But there was also no way he was giving up on them. He'd fight to the death to keep her and the kids.

They drove in heavy silence to his hotel and he led her up to his room. He'd just fished William's flash drive out of his pocket to plug into his laptop when Laura's cell phone rang. He frowned. It was nearly 2 a.m. Who'd call her at this time of night? Was it Adam, waking up from a nightmare and needing his mother's voice to comfort him? Guilt at tearing Laura away from their son speared through him.

But then he heard a shrill female voice babbling through the line and Laura's face drained of all color. Panic unlike anything he'd ever experienced before, including the moments after he first woke up in his box, ripped through him. Adam. Oh, God. What had happened to his son?

Laura was going to throw up. "What have you done?" she gasped in a horrible, unrecognizable voice at Nick. She shoved past him and ran for the toilet in the tiny connected bathroom.

"What happened? What's going on?" Nick demanded right on her heels. "Whatever I've done, I'll fix it. I swear."

"They've kidnapped him," she sobbed. "Adam and Lisbet are gone. Marta was drugged and just woke up. The police are at the house and the FBI's been called." Her stomach rebelled then, and she emptied what little she'd had for dinner into the toilet.

Ice-cold terror washed over Nick's face. "Is there a ransom note?"

"No." Laura splashed cold water on her

face. It didn't do a thing to drive back the nausea washing through her. She rinsed her mouth and headed into the bedroom.

"What else did Marta say?" Nick demanded.

"That's it. Adam and his nanny are gone. There are signs of a struggle in the playroom. Lisbet must have put up a fight. The kidnappers have a six-hour head start and could be anywhere by now."

She couldn't stand still and moved around the room searching it frantically for she knew not what. Nick finally caught her in his arms and held her board-stiff body tightly against his until the worst of her panic passed.

"They've got my baby," she wailed. "He must be so scared. If they hurt him—" she broke off on a sob "—oh, God."

"I'll kill Meredith if she's behind this," Nick gritted out.

Laura was swinging back and forth between terror and rage so fast she could hardly keep up with it. She gazed up at Nick with tears streaming down her cheeks. "What do we do?"

He gripped her shoulders tightly and stared into her stricken gaze, clearly willing her to hold it together. "We fight. We do whatever it takes to find him and get him back safe and sound."

Under his hands, she squared her shoulders. "You're right. Nobody's messing with my baby and getting away with it." Death dripped in her voice. Super Mommy had just gone over to the dark side. Whoever'd kidnapped Adam was going to pay in blood. She *would* find her son and get him back.

Perceptive as ever, Ellie started to fuss in the crib in the corner.

Nick suggested, "You take care of Ellie. I'll make the arrangements to get back home."

Laura nodded and stumbled to the crib the hotel had sent up while Nick called the airport and hired a private jet to take them back to Washington with all possible haste.

Nick joined her in the bedroom. "A plane

will be ready in an hour. We've got about twenty minutes before we have to leave for the airport. The concierge will have a taxi waiting for us downstairs."

Ellie's tiny body snuggling tightly against hers calmed Laura enough that she could begin to think rationally. When the baby had fallen asleep in her arms, she said quietly, "I'm not entirely sure your wife is behind this. At least not directly."

"Why's that?" Nick asked in surprise over his shoulder as he threw his things into his suitcase.

"If she was involved in your original kidnapping, surely she was told when you were rescued. Which means she's had a year to react to your escape. Why this, why now?"

"If she was involved with my kidnapping, then she'd have known I suffered a memory loss. If I didn't come forward for a year, she might have figured I was never going to identify myself as Nikolas Spiros."

"Either way," Laura reasoned aloud, "she

had no reason to believe you were ever coming back. Why would she have planned an elaborate kidnapping of your son? Because believe me—nobody got through my house's security without some serious planning."

Nick made a rueful face. "Maybe she found out I'd visited my old attorney and figured I was going to make a run at getting my company back."

Laura thought aloud. "Okay. She had a motive to grab Adam. But still. Just a few days to hire a kidnapper, get him in place, find your son, figure out how to get past my estate's formidable security, and execute a kidnapping? That's just not plausible."

"Who else could it be?"

She answered grimly, "It's not like you and I don't have other enemies. What about AbaCo? Could they be trying to blackmail you into not testifying against them?"

Fury glittered in Nick's gaze. "They most certainly have experience with kidnapping and the personnel to pull one off on short notice. And they know you and the children are my life. But going after a child? Those bastards…" His voice trailed off as he choked on his fury.

She knew the feeling. "The trial starts next week. If they have Adam, we're going to have to find him fast."

"I know just the person to ask if AbaCo has Adam."

"Who?"

"AbaCo's CEO."

"Werner Kloffman?" Laura echoed. "Where on earth would we find him? High-profile people like him tend to move around the globe and don't exactly advertise their whereabouts."

"What do you want to bet he's in Washington pulling strings and trying to get the government to drop its case against his company?"

"Good point. If you'll step aside and give me access to your laptop, MysteryMom needs to contact a few strategically placed people within the government."

"MysteryMom?" Nick asked.

"That's my email handle when I'm doing work for DaddyFinders, Inc. I built up a pretty decent informant network over my years of searching for you."

He looked at her soberly. "I am eternally grateful you never gave up on me. You and I won't give up on Adam, either. We'll find him."

A sob threatened to erupt from her chest, but she shoved it down. Her baby boy needed Super Mommy firing on all cylinders right now.

Nick must have sensed her momentary weakness because he said encouragingly, "Lisbet's with him. She'll protect him as fiercely as you would."

She nodded gamely, refraining from sug-gesting that Lisbet might very well be dead and out of the picture by now. She knew all too well how important it was not to dwell on the negative, but instead to focus on hope and determination and keep moving forward.

Nick's arms came around her. She clung to him tightly. Despite the unresolved problems between them, they were united in purpose when it came to retrieving their son. And that was all that mattered for now.

She disentangled herself from his arms and headed for Nick's laptop computer.

Nick woke up as gray dawn crept around the jet's window blinds, surprised that he'd managed to catch a nap. Fear for Adam slammed into him moments after his eyes blinked open, so heavy on his chest that he could hardly breathe. He tossed and turned in the uncomfortable airplane seat, tearing himself apart with guilt over having brought this danger to his son. Thankfully, Laura was asleep stretched out across several seats and Ellie was crashed in a playpen. He slipped out of his seat and tiptoed over to check on

Ellie. The poor baby'd had a rough night last night and was sleeping deeply.

This aircraft was equipped with Wi-Fi, and he used it to connect his laptop to the internet and check the morning news. The gossip sites were having a field day over his return to the public eye. Even serious news outlets were commenting freely on the status of the Spiros fortune now that Nikolas Spiros was back. Analysts were speculating gleefully on whether he would attempt to seize control of his company from the German firm that had owned it for the past half-dozen years.

A limousine met them at the airport when they landed and whisked them south to Laura's estate in Virginia. The mansion was crawling with police and FBI investigators who had frustratingly little information to share about Adam and Lisbet's disappearance. The FBI kidnapping expert on scene seemed alarmed by the lack of a ransom note.

When Laura pushed the fellow to speculate

on who'd taken her son, the FBI man hinted that perhaps whoever'd taken Adam didn't feel a need to leave a note but felt the message was loud and clear enough without one.

Nick's jaw tightened grimly. Which was a fancy way of the guy saying he thought AbaCo had Adam and that the kidnapper's intent was clear—stop the child's father from testifying against the company.

It didn't help matters that, by midafternoon, the estate's front gate was crowded with luridly curious reporters. The FBI had felt it would be best to go public with the story, plastering the news with pictures of Adam and putting the public on notice to look out for the little boy. It was a close call to say who hated the media attention more—him or Laura. Both of them were stretched to the breaking point by the lack of progress and the feeling of being trapped in their own home.

Finally, as they picked at the sandwiches a red-eyed Marta put in front of them, Laura's laptop beeped to indicate an incoming message. She leaped from her seat to check it.

"It's for MysteryMom," she said tersely as she opened the message. Instinct had warned her not to reveal all her sources to the FBI team that had invaded their home. She'd kept her MysteryMom identity and email account to herself since the FBI was monitoring all her phones and other email accounts. Nick moved to her side quickly. The message, short and to the point, popped up. Kloffman is borrowing a home from friends at the following address. A posh street in the Washington, D.C. suburb, Old Town Alexandria, was named. The message was not signed. Not that he cared who had sent it, other than to want to thank the person someday…after Adam was safe.

Laura murmured under her breath, "We'll have to sneak out past the FBI and the police."

He nodded slightly. "I'll engage them in

conversation while you make arrangements for Ellie."

He went downstairs and didn't engage in conversation as much as he threw a tantrum, demanding that the law enforcement agencies *do* something. Personally, he understood that they had no leads to go on and their hands were tied until the kidnapper made the next move. But he kept that opinion to himself as he ranted and generally forced everyone's attention onto him while Laura had a quiet word with Marta about watching Ellie for the night and milk in the freezer.

Laura slipped into the living room and made eye contact with him. He allowed her to talk him down off his fake ledge and the police were more than happy to let the two of them retire upstairs to the privacy of their suite.

"Are we good to go?" he asked Laura when the door shut behind her.

"Yes."

He eyed the black turtleneck and slacks

she'd laid out on the bed. "I gather you're planning to break into the guy's house?" he asked doubtfully.

"Do you have a better idea?" she demanded.

"Actually, yes." He headed for her closet and pulled out an elegant linen sheath dress, silk stockings, fashionable stilettos, and an expensive pearl necklace. "Put these on. And do up your makeup and hair to the hilt."

"What do you have in mind?"

"Let's knock on his front door. Or more precisely, you knock on the front door. He won't think twice about opening the door for a woman who looks like you. Once he's got the door open, I'll join you. If we have to force our way in after that, so be it. But I bet he doesn't put up a fight. He's a business-man, not a thug."

"You're probably right. I'm not thinking all that clearly right now." She glanced at him gratefully, and the spark of warmth in her eyes shot through him like a lightning bolt.

Even in the midst of this crisis, she attracted him like no other woman.

She was authorized to be off her A-game. It was no surprise she'd fall back on her old CIA habits in a situation like this. But he knew life as a CEO. And if a beautiful, elegant woman showed up at his front door, he'd have let her in.

Laura dressed quickly and came back into the sitting room looking like a million bucks. Her flesh impact hit him like a physical blow. "You're a hell of a woman," he murmured.

"I'm a freaked-out mommy."

"Stay strong, sweetheart. For Adam."

She nodded and stepped close, leaning against him. They stood together quietly for a moment.

"Ready?" he murmured.

"Let's do it."

It was ridiculously easy to sneak out of their house. Laura knew every detail of the security system and made easy work of slipping past it. They pushed his BMW out of the garage in neutral and let it roll down the slight hill behind the house until it was out of sight of the mansion. Only then did Nick start the engine and guide the vehicle toward the back gate.

The trip to the Virginia suburbs of D.C. went quickly. Laura was grim and silent beside him. She definitely had her Super Mommy game face on.

The GPS efficiently led them to an elegantly restored row house in the heart of Old Town. Nick pulled into a driveway a few houses down and turned off the engine. He murmured, "You go first and I'll lurk in the bushes until Kloffman has opened the door."

Laura nodded coldly. Super Mommy was in full grizzly-bear mode. Satisfaction coursed through him. AbaCo's senior leadership had coming whatever Laura could dish out and then some.

He followed her to the front porch and crouched beside the lush rhododendrons flanking the front steps. She rang the bell and stepped back so she'd be in plain sight through the door's peephole.

The door opened.

Laura pitched her voice in a sexy contralto. "Mr. Kloffman? I work for the United States government. Do you have a few minutes to speak with me?"

"Of course. Please come in."

Bingo. Show time.

Chapter 8

Laura was surprised at how easily it all came back to her—the technical skill, intense focus, the cold calm. Her mindset also included absolute willingness to do whatever violence was necessary to find and rescue her son.

As she passed through the front door, she placed her shoe strategically in front of the wood panel. Nick materialized behind her and had slipped inside before Kloffman was even aware of the man behind her.

"Who in the hell are you?" Kloffman growled as he caught sight of Nick.

"My name's Nikolas Spiros, Herr Kloffman."

The German spluttered, looking back and forth between the two of them. "You! I thought I recognized you. You're that Delaney woman."

"That's correct," Laura answered grimly. "We need to chat, sir."

"How dare you? How did you find me? I want my lawyer."

"This isn't that kind of chat, Werner," Nick said in an entirely too pleasant tone of voice. "Shall we step into the living room?"

The German must have sensed the threat underlying Nick's words and moved without comment into an antique-filled parlor. A thrill coursed through her at the danger in Nick's voice. She remembered sharply why she'd been attracted to him in the first place. It had been this sense of sexy risk that had clung to him.

Kloffman sank down in a wingback chair and stared defiantly at the two of them.

"So here's the deal, Werner," Laura said reasonably. "We're going to ask you a series of questions. If you give us the right answers, we'll leave and not bother you again. If you give us the wrong answers, you are going to have a very long night. We'd like to keep this civilized, but we are under no obligation to do so. Understood?"

Kloffman swore under his breath in German. "I know who you are. I'll see you both in jail for this."

Nick shrugged. "Panicked parents politely question the man most likely to have kidnapped their son, and you think any jury in the world is going to do more than slap our wrists?"

"I didn't kidnap your son!"

"Of course you didn't," she replied smoothly. "The same way you didn't kidnap Nick. Your flunkies did it for you. Plausible deniability is important for a man in your position, is it not?"

He shrugged, obviously aware that answering the question couldn't help his cause.

"Surely you knew about Nick's kidnapping and the kidnappings of dozens of other people who were held aboard your ships. It must have been a profitable little side business. What were you getting for your special guest service? A million dollars a year per prisoner? More?"

Nick stiffened beside her. His rage was palpable at being in the presence of the man who very likely was the kingpin behind his kidnapping.

"Care to comment on who paid to have Nick kidnapped?" she asked without warning.

Kloffman's gaze darted back and forth between them. He definitely knew something he wasn't sharing with them.

"His loving wife, perhaps?" Laura snapped.

"I have no idea." Kloffman's eyes slid down and to the left, a sure tell that he was lying.

Laura leaned in close. "Was it her? Yes or no."

"No." Another glance at the floor and a jump of the pulse pounding in his temple.

She looked up at Nick grimly. "At least that mystery's solved. It was your bitch of a wife." She looked back down at Kloffman. "Where's our son?"

"Why would I kidnap some child?" Kloffman demanded angrily. "I'm not a monster."

"Five years in a box on one of your ships says that's not true," Nick snarled.

Kloffman subsided, glaring belligerently.

Laura spoke grimly. "The fact remains that no one but you has both the means and the motive to kidnap our son and pressure Nick not to testify against your firm. AbaCo's going down in flames next week and Nick is the spark that's going to ignite the firestorm."

Kloffman smiled coldly. "AbaCo is by no means going down in flames. Quite the contrary."

A chill passed down her spine. The German was entirely too sure of himself for her comfort. He should be sweating bullets if he was involved in Adam's kidnapping. But instead, he was sitting here as smug as could be, actually smirking at her.

She pulled out her pistol, and it had the desired effect on Kloffman. He paled. She spoke grimly. "Convince me why I should believe that you and AbaCo had nothing to do with our son's disappearance."

Kloffman's lips pressed tightly shut and she leaned forward, caressing his cheek with the barrel of the weapon. Her voice was velvet. "You see, Herr Kloffman. I'm a mother. And if something bad happens to my baby boy, I'm not going to give a damn whether or not I live or die. It won't matter to me one bit if I rot in jail for the rest of my life. So I have nothing to lose by putting a bullet through your knee—or through your head."

Kloffman began to tremble and a fat bead of sweat ran down the side of his face. Now he was getting into the proper spirit of things.

"I swear. I had nothing to do with your son's kidnapping."

Nick replied tersely, "Convince us you and your goons didn't do it."

Kloffman stammered, "I'm sure nobody in the firm would do such a thing without my approval."

Nick leaped all over that. "So you're admitting that no major black ops happen at AbaCo without your knowledge?"

"Are you kidding?"

Kloffman looked like he'd blurted that out without thinking. He fell silent and a thoughtful look entered his eyes. She gave him as long as he wanted to work through whatever was on his mind. Nick also looked inclined to let the man stew in his thoughts for the time being.

Eventually, Kloffman said heavily, "Many things happen without my knowledge at AbaCo. I'm purely a figurehead around there."

Laura stared. The statement had a definite ring of truth to it. The guy was a figurehead? "Who's the real power at AbaCo, then?"

Kloffman glared at Nick. "As Ms. Delaney put it so succinctly, a cabal of criminals put in place by your bitch of a wife."

"Can you prove that?" Laura demanded.

"Why should I?" Kloffman shot back.

She considered him carefully. "Because I'll hold you responsible for kidnapping my son and kill you if you don't?"

He let out an exasperated sigh. "Look. They pay me a small fortune to be the public face of AbaCo. But I'm not about to go down in flames, as you say, for all the activities they're into."

Nick leaped on that right away. "What else is AbaCo up to besides human trafficking?"

Kloffman snorted. "That's the tip of the iceberg."

Laura had no trouble believing that. "Again, I ask if you have any proof."

"Why should I hand any of it over to you?"

Nick asked reasonably, "Who else would you give it to? If you were going to hand it over to the U.S. government, you'd have done it before now—when it became clear the feds are going to come after AbaCo with everything they've got in the upcoming trial. But you saw what Meredith's goons did to me. I think you're afraid to cross her. And rightly so, by the way."

Nick was doing an excellent job of playing good cop. Which left her to play bad cop.

She leaned forward. "Don't be stupid, Werner. I have the gun, and I won't hesitate to use it."

The German looked back and forth between them. "Let me make a phone call to inquire about your boy."

She considered briefly. Why not? What could it hurt? She nodded and allowed the man to pull out a cell phone. He put it on speaker and laid it on the coffee table in front of him before hitting a speed dial number.

Nick commented as a man's voice came on the line, "I speak fluent German."

She threw him a grateful look. That could prove immensely helpful.

Kloffman nodded irritably at them. "Klaus. It's Kloffman. Did you hear that Nick Cass's boy was kidnapped?"

"It's all over the news," a heavily accented voice replied in English. "Serves the bastard right."

Kloffman asked, "Do you know anything about it that could implicate AbaCo?"

"No." The guy sounded genuinely surprised. "We had no such orders. Besides, everyone would suspect us right away. We're not that stupid. Just do what you were sent to Washington to do and stay out of things that don't concern you."

Laura was surprised by the scorn in this Klaus guy's voice. That didn't sound anything at all like the respect due a genuine CEO. She glanced over at Nick and he was frowning, too. Apparently, Werner was telling the truth about being a figurehead.

"I'm sorry to bother you, Klaus."

The German ended the call. "Satisfied?" Kloffman spit out.

She answered, "Not yet."

"Look. I have children of my own. I would not hurt your son." As her gaze hardened, he added in desperation, "Why would I kidnap your boy? The trial's going to be stopped anyway."

Laura started, and it was Nick who leaned forward and said smoothly, "Who did you cut the deal with, Werner?"

"The CIA."

Laura was stunned. Her own agency had sold her out?

Thankfully, Nick didn't miss a beat and nodded beside her. "Of course. I'll bet you've held a few prisoners for the agency, maybe given them a heads-up where certain ship-ments were headed. You scratch their back, and now you've called in the favor and forced them to scratch yours."

"Exactly," Kloffman exclaimed, obviously relieved that Nick was on the same page. "In another day or two, the federal prosecutors will announce that national security could be compromised by proceeding with the case, and all charges will be quietly dropped. I have no need to kidnap your boy to silence you."

Then why did Meredith and the shadow operators at AbaCo go after Adam? Petty revenge? The question still remained as to how they'd managed to move so fast against her heavily defended estate. It just didn't add up in Laura's gut. She was missing something major, here.

Nick, bless him, was carrying the conversation while her mind stayed frustratingly blank. He asked the German, "When will the announcement be made stopping the trial?"

"Two days from now."

Laura's heart sank. If AbaCo was behind his kidnapping, they had two days before Adam's life became irrelevant to his kidnappers. How were they ever going to find him in so little time? Worse, if the trial was dead in the water, she and Nick had no leverage whatsoever to force this man to help them find Adam. Unless…

She leaned forward. "Werner, here's the deal. Even if the trial is halted, Nick and I aren't going to stop. We're going to go public with everything we have on your company. We'll use the media to full advantage, and with what we've got on AbaCo, we'll destroy the company. In fact, we can probably do a more effective job of ruining it without the constraints of a trial to tie our hands. Do you believe me?"

Kloffman stared at her for several long seconds. Finally, he said heavily, "What's it going to take to stop you from doing that?"

He might be a figurehead, but he undoubtedly liked his paycheck. He also seemed to understand that, as the figurehead, he'd be the sacrificial lamb.

Nick replied gently, "Save yourself, Werner. You don't strike me as a bad type. Don't let Meredith and her cronies drag you down with them."

"How?" Werner snapped. "Who'll believe me?"

"Why wouldn't people believe you?" Nick asked. "I'm living proof that someone at AbaCo is up to no good. And there are others who have been victims of the company."

Werner shook his head. "You don't understand. It's not about the prisoners they keep. It's about the cargo."

Nick glanced at her. Werner seemed inclined to talk to Nick, so she nodded subtly at him to take the lead. "What about the cargo?" Nick asked.

"AbaCo has become the freight carrier of choice for every nefarious group you can think of—drug lords, weapons dealers, terrorists, slavers, illegal lumber smugglers, you name it."

Nick paled beside her. It had to be painful to hear that his family's firm had fallen so far. "Do you have proof?" he asked hoarsely.

Kloffman hesitated one last time, and then he capitulated all in a rush. "I've been collecting it for years. Bit by bit. I had to be careful. But I've got cargo manifests, incriminating emails from customers, shipping documents, even financial records."

"Why haven't you taken it to the authorities before now?" Nick queried.

"What authorities?" Kloffman answered bitterly. "The same ones who are also using AbaCo to do their dirty work? How do you think the CIA gets weapons and supplies to the various regimes Uncle Sam can't publicly support?"

The three of them fell silent.

Laura eventually broke the silence. "Who within the company does the dirty work?"

"The Special Cargo division," Kloffman answered promptly.

That made sense. The people on trial for kidnapping Nick came out of that group. But the Feds had been combing through that division's records for most of the past year and not found anything to indicate that

AbaCo was engaging in widespread criminal activity.

"Do you have access to their real records, then?" Laura asked curiously.

Kloffman nodded eagerly. "I've been copying everything for the past three years." He added sourly, "They didn't even bother to restrict my access to the accounts. They think I'm too stupid to notice what they're up to."

Nick made a commiserating sound, and Werner shared an aggrieved look with him. Nick really was incredible at garnering empathy and trust from the German. He asked gently, "Do you have copies of these records with you? If you wouldn't mind sharing them with us, I swear to you we'll see they fall into the right hands."

Kloffman reared back sharply. "No way. They'll kill me."

No need to ask who "they" was. Nick said soothingly, "Not if they don't know who the source of the leak was. I give you my word of honor we won't reveal where or who we got the information from."

Kloffman didn't look convinced. Laura spoke quietly. "Somebody has kidnapped our son. He's six years old. And he's going to die if we don't find him. Soon. Please help us, Herr Kloffman. I promise we'll help you."

He nodded slowly. "I will give you everything I have. Maybe you can find something about your boy."

Laura rose to her feet eagerly and Nick did the same.

"I'm sorry, but I don't have the files with me. I keep them in a safe place."

As would she in the same situation. So. It was going to require a leap of faith on their part, too. "Of course, Herr Kloffman. How soon can you get us a copy?"

"Twenty-four hours, maybe."

A whole day? Her gut twisted in dismay. But it wasn't like she had any choice in the matter. "Please hurry." Desperation crept into her voice. "He's so little…."

Kloffman squeezed her elbow reassuringly. "I shall do what I can to help, *Fraulein.*"

She nodded, too choked up to say any more. Nick quietly traded contact information with the German and then guided her to the front door.

"A word of advice, Kloffman," Nick commented as he reached for the doorknob. "Convince whoever's actually running the show to sell off the pre-1970 ships before you have a major accident. Dump the Euro debt and invest in new, Norwegian-built, fast ships."

Kloffman stared. "I beg your pardon?"

Nick shrugged. "Spiros Shipping has been in my family for three generations. And it's being run into the ground. Stop thinking about short-term profit and look to the future before you destroy my company."

The German stared, flummoxed. "Assuming I still have a job in a week, I'll try."

"Thank you for your help, Herr Kloffman,"

Nick said soberly as he opened the front door. "We are in your debt."

Out of reflex, Laura reached for the light switch and turned off the porch light as she stepped outside. The night was dark and cold, and she was more terrified than ever of the forces that had taken her son from her.

Chapter 9

Nick's breathing still hadn't returned to normal, and he'd been driving as fast as he dared back toward the estate for nearly a half hour. His company had become a major crime syndicate, compliments of a wife he didn't remember? Why on God's green earth had he ever married the woman? He supposed it didn't matter, now. The deed was done, the damage cascading down on everyone he loved.

Laura burst out, "Do we dare trust him? With Adam's life?"

"I think we should," he answered.

"Why?"

He shrugged. "The time may come when we need Kloffman to hesitate before he calls his dogs down on us or Adam. I think we gave him good reason to hesitate."

Laura sighed beside him. "You're right, of course. I'm just not capable of thinking that clearly right now."

He glanced over at her. "You're not supposed to be thinking clearly. You're a mother. You're allowed to be panicked."

"But Adam needs Super Mommy." Laura's voice cracked, sending a glass shard of pain through him. How was she ever going to move past the fact that he'd done this to their child? Even assuming Adam returned home safe and sound—and he refused to consider any other possibility—how were they going to move forward as a couple?

He asked slowly, "Do think you'll ever forgive me for all of this?"

She stared across the dark interior of the car at him a long time before she answered. "I don't know. After you lied to me in Paris and then spent the past year knowing you were living under an assumed identity and never told me, I don't know how I'm going to trust you again."

If only he could remember why he'd deceived her in Paris! For the first time, he regretted not really trying to work with the doctors who'd attempted to help him regain his memory.

"Now what?" Laura asked.

What, indeed? He was as stymied as she was and hated feeling this helpless. He'd felt this way in his box and had vowed never to be at anyone's mercy again. No, this time it was his son's life on the line. His control threatened to crack. Swearing silently, he fought off the urge. Laura needed him strong. Adam needed him strong.

"I don't have a lot of contacts in the crime world," Laura commented, "but I'll put out some feelers. See if anyone's heard anything."

"I'd lay odds that whoever kidnapped me

grabbed Adam, too," Nick declared. "I'd love nothing better than to get my hands on that person and wring their neck."

"You only want to wring their neck? I had something slower and more painful in mind," Laura replied.

He shrugged. "I got you and the kids out of the deal. I learned things about myself in that box I'd have learned no other way. Things that have changed my life—changed me—dramatically for the better. Yes, the experience sucked. But, at some point, I have to get over it and get on with my life. I'm not kidding when I say that part of my past is over and gone. I don't dwell on it."

"I'm not so altruistic," Laura muttered.

"You can sit around hating your life and bemoaning all your problems. Or you can accept that everyone has them and get on with dealing with yours in a positive frame of mind. I'm not saying life can't be hard as hell. But it is possible to find joy in small things in the midst of all the bad stuff. I have my kidnapper to thank for making me understand this."

"Will you be so philosophical if we find out he or she is behind Adam's kidnapping?"

"I'll kill him." He added grimly, "And I'll be entirely philosophical about it afterward."

Laura smiled reluctantly and reached over to put a hand on his leg. He took a hand off the steering wheel and covered hers.

"We'll find Adam," Nick murmured. "Just keep the faith." Why did it take something so awful to bring them together like this? How was he supposed to feel anything other than too guilty to breathe when he was finding Laura again in the midst of losing his son?

The house was in an uproar when they walked in. Marta had gone upstairs for Ellie's 2 a.m. feeding and one of the FBI agents had discovered their disappearance.

The FBI agent-in-charge, a guy named Cal Blackledge, was not amused and chewed them up one side and down the other. Nick blandly explained that the two of them had needed to get away for a little while, to be alone and share their grief without an army of onlookers. Blackledge didn't look convinced, but Nick and Laura stuck to their story, and there wasn't much the FBI man could do about it.

As their chewing out was winding down, another FBI agent rushed into the kitchen. "You just got a message from who we believe to be the kidnapper."

Laura's coffee mug slipped out of her fingers and shattered into a hundred pieces all over the floor. Nick moved for the door nearly as quickly as she did, but Blackledge still got to Laura's office first. When Nick stepped into the spacious room, a team of people was huddling in front of her computer. They moved aside, and Laura slipped into her desk chair. He watched eagerly as she clicked on the email message.

Your son and his nanny are safe. They will stay with me until you testify against

AbaCo. When those bastards are put away for good, then you can have your son back. Do not fail, or else.

Laura looked up at him in shock, the thought plain on her face the same as the one he was having. *The kidnapper was an enemy of AbaCo's?*

He asked, "What's the kidnapper going to do when the government announces that it's going to drop its charges?"

Laura paled and started to shake. He knew the feeling, dammit. They had two days until Adam's life was forfeit. Two days to find and save their son.

Nick had faced some scary crises in his life, but nothing compared to this. His son's life was in mortal danger. Seeing the threat on the computer screen before him made it real in a way it hadn't been until now. Nausea ripped through him.

"There's a video attachment," one of the FBI agents announced.

Laura clicked on it. A picture of their son smiling up at the camera flashed onto the computer monitor. The video rolled and Adam placed a bright red leaf into what looked like some kind of scrapbook. "Look at my pretty leaf," he announced in his clear, sweet voice.

Lisbet's voice came from off camera. "Tell Mummy and Daddy we're doing fine and that you're safe and warm and well-fed. Tell them Joe has been *très* kind to us."

Adam nodded. "I'm learning all kinds of neat things about nature. But I miss you. Joe says you're fighting the bad man for him. Hurry up and win. I want to go home."

A sob escaped Laura and she turned to Nick, burying her face against his side. He gripped her shoulder so tightly he was probably hurting her. But he couldn't help himself.

The FBI agents went into high gear around them.

"Identify that leaf."

"Nature. He's being held in a rural area."

"Joe. Get a list of disgruntled former AbaCo employees."

"The child turned the page in that album. Can we digitally enhance the leaves on the second page?"

"Analyze the grain of the floorboards. They look old. Rough. Maybe in a cabin of some kind."

The words flowed past Nick, but the only ones that stuck were the final ones in the note. Do not fail or else.

Or else.

Laura lifted her head. "Lisbet used the French word for very, *très*. She doesn't speak much French. She was signaling us that the kidnapper is French or speaks French."

Blackledge snapped, "Make that a list of French former AbaCo employees."

A flurry of phone calls took place around them while Laura replayed the video over and over, presumably looking for more clues. Or maybe she just needed to see Adam's face. It was both sweet relief and stabbing pain to see him. He might be safe for now, but that *or else* hung heavily over the little boy.

"AbaCo is refusing to release any employee lists to us without a subpoena."

"Then get one," Blackledge snapped.

"That's going to be a problem," someone replied. "They'll have to release information about their American staff to us, but not their overseas employees."

Blackledge frowned. "The French courts are notoriously slow, particularly when it comes to cooperating with Americans. We're not exactly at the top of France's list of allies these days. If AbaCo refuses to cooperate, it's going to take too long to get what we need."

Nick said sharply, "Spiros Shipping had a major office in Paris. AbaCo probably still uses it."

"Do you think Kloffman—" Laura started.

Nick cut her off gently. "Why go to the top when you can go to the bottom?"

She frowned at him and he explained, "I ran Spiros Shipping for well over a decade. I'm betting Kloffman didn't fire every one of my old employees when AbaCo took over. People who used to work for me must still be there."

"What good does that do us?" she asked.

"My family believed strongly in knowing every employee and in building trust and loyalty among them. If I can find some of the old staff, they'll help me."

She pulled out her cell phone and slapped it into his hand.

"Let's see if they bothered to change the phone numbers," he muttered. He dialed the international number for Spiros Paris and was pleased when the call went through.

"AbaCo Shipping," a female voice said in his ear.

"Marie? Marie Clothier? Is that you?"

She switched into English to match his. "*Oui*. Who may I ask, is this?"

"Nick—" Then he corrected, "Nikolas Spiros."

The woman took off in a spate of excited French he only half caught. When she'd finally wound down, he said, "Look, Marie. I need your help. My son has been kidnapped and we're trying to figure out who did it. I need a list of all the employees fired from the Paris office since AbaCo took over. Is there someone left from the old days who would do that for me? Quietly and quickly?"

"But of course. Let me connect you with François Guerrard."

Nick laughed. "He's still working? Why didn't he retire years ago?"

"He would have if AbaCo hadn't cut our pensions so badly."

"Ahh, I'm sorry. I suppose it goes without saying that it would be best for you if you didn't mention this little call to anyone at AbaCo?"

She laughed wryly. "That would be correct, sir. Ahh, it is so good to hear your voice again. I never believed what they said about you—"

He gently cut off what was likely to become a lengthy monologue from the talkative woman. "Thank you, Marie. I'm afraid I'm in a great hurry. We need to find my son."

"Of course, Monsieur Nikolas. I shall pray for him."

In a few minutes, a list of fired employees was sitting in his email inbox. Blackledge printed it out and his people went to work tracking down every single person on the list. Nick and Laura stayed out of the way and let the FBI invoke its formidable connections with Interpol to do the job.

The leaves were identified as belonging to plants indigenous to the mid-Atlantic states. Nick supposed knowing Adam was in one of a half-dozen states was better than nothing, but not much.

Laura spoke to Nick thoughtfully. "Why did Lisbet make a point of saying they were warm? It has been unseasonably warm all over the East Coast this past week. Is there somewhere substantially colder within this region that would prompt her comment?"

"Mountains or a coast," Nick replied.

Laura turned to one of the FBI agents. "Would those leaves we saw be more likely to grow at high elevations or near the ocean?"

"The second leaf is a bush that tolerates salt spray well, ma'am."

"The shore it is," Laura announced.

Blackledge nodded his agreement. "You sure you don't want back into this business, ma'am?"

She laughed without much humor. "Just get my son back so I can be a mommy."

Nick put an arm around her shoulders and was gratified when she leaned against him. Within the hour, hundreds of law enforcement officials were combing the woods of coastal Virginia, searching for an isolated cabin. It was a needle-in-a-haystack hunt, but he appreciated the effort nonetheless.

A command center was set up in their

living room to coordinate the various search teams, and he and Laura were only in the way. They eventually retreated to their suite to let Blackledge's team do its job.

It was late afternoon when Nick's phone dinged to indicate an incoming text message. He checked it quickly. "Kloffman. He wants to meet us in Washington tonight. Says he'll have what we need then. Do you think Agent Blackledge will lynch us if we sneak out again?"

She answered gravely, "I do. I'd suggest we tell him what we're up to this time." Their gazes met in mutual understanding. This was one of those times when no words were necessary for them to communicate perfectly.

Nick nodded. His thoughts drifted to his wife, Meredith, and the roadblock she represented to his future with Laura. "You do know that the minute I'm clear of her, I'm going to ask you to marry me, right?"

"And you're so sure I'll say yes?" Laura replied tightly.

He stared, thunderstruck. "You wouldn't marry me?"

"Nick, my son is gone. Everything I thought I knew about you turns out to be a lie. You have a *wife*. You cheated on her with me in Paris."

"Everything I know of her says I barely knew her and she no doubt married me purely for my money. There's no way it was a love match."

"I don't care how good or bad she was. You broke your marriage vows. I have a problem with that."

"I don't remember any of it," he replied with barely restrained frustration. "I can't imagine ever having married her. And even if I actually thought it was a good idea at some point, I'm not that man anymore."

"It's a lot for me to accept on faith."

"Laura, I love you with all my heart. Adam *will* come home safe and sound. This crisis will pass, and I'll still love you. I'll love you till the end of time."

"Is love enough?" she asked in anguish. "I'm not so sure."

"Love is everything," he replied with a desperate calm that belied the panic beneath.

Without replying, she turned and walked out of the room. His heart broke a little more. He had to find a way to put his family back together. There *had* to be a way.

How was it she could feel like she was drowning even though she wasn't even in water? Laura's world had come apart and she didn't have any idea how to put it back together again. She'd have thought her stress would have gone down slightly after the note from the kidnapper. The FBI profilers were confident that Adam wasn't in any immediate danger, and whoever had him was on their side in the fight against AbaCo. That had to count for something, right?

But instead, she could hardly function. Her thoughts were disjointed, she was unable to plan anything, and even the smallest of tasks overwhelmed her. Only Ellie kept her sane. The infant adhered to a steady schedule of eating, cuddling, and sleeping, and Laura was immensely grateful for the infant's rhythms.

It took twice as long as usual, but eventually, Laura formed a plan of action. First on her agenda was to contact some people at the CIA and see if Kloffman's claims were true. Had the agency cut a deal with him to block the AbaCo trial from going forward in the name of national security? If so, she planned to pull every string she had at her disposal to get the CIA to delay making the announcement for a few more days.

Laura slept restlessly in the recliner in Ellie's room, waking up a little after dawn. She pulled out her cell phone and dialed a familiar phone number. The CIA operator forwarded her call to her old boss.

"Hi, Clifton, it's Laura Delaney."

"I wondered how long it was going to take you to call me."

"So it's true? There's a deal to stop the AbaCo trial?"

"You know I'm not allowed to comment on such things, dear."

"And you understand the life of an innocent child is on the line?"

He sighed. "I do. I was so sorry to hear about the kidnapping. Is there any ransom demand?"

She replied sharply, "Why, yes. There is. The kidnapper is insisting that Nick testify against AbaCo and bury them, or else."

Heavy silence greeted that announcement. It was all the answer she needed from Clifton. The CIA had, indeed, cut a deal with AbaCo. "When is it going public?" she asked. "And don't tell me that information is classified. We have to find Adam before the news is released."

"Close of business today."

It wasn't enough time! "You have to delay it. We have to find my son first!"

"I understand, Laura. I'll see what I can do. But I can't make any promises."

She hung up, staring in dismay at the happy clouds and dancing unicorns on Ellie's pink walls. Adam was running out of time.

The FBI upped the man power over the course of the day, redoubling their efforts to locate Adam, but to no avail. Wherever the kidnapper was hiding him, he'd picked his spot well.

It was afternoon when another email came to her Laura Delaney address from the kidnapper. She raced downstairs and into the office to see it. Nick was already there, and he smiled encouragingly at her. Did that mean there was good news?

She sat down at her desk and read the note:

Thought you might like another video to know your son's okay. I promise I won't hurt him as long as you do the right thing and send AbaCo to hell where it belongs.

The attached video showed Adam playing some sort of pick-up-sticks game with Lisbet and squealing with laughter. For a kidnapping victim, he looked shockingly hale and hearty. The FBI team observing with her murmured in surprise.

"What?" she looked up at the faces around her in concern.

Blackledge shook his head. "This is the damnedest case. I've never seen a kid having the time of his life being kidnapped."

"Stockholm syndrome?" another agent suggested.

Laura frowned. Stockholm syndrome was when kidnapping victims began to sympathize with their captors. It was an involuntary psychological reaction to the threat of dying.

Blackledge replied, "I don't think so. The kid and nanny look like they're genuinely having a ball."

Laura asked, "Are they just making the best of a bad situation?"

One of the other analysts leaned forward, watching a playback of the tape. "They're showing no stress-related body language. The muscles of the nanny's face are relaxed and open, and see the way Adam's lounging, here? He's not taking any sort of self-protective posture. These two feel completely safe with their captor."

Another agent piped up. "In both notes, the kidnapper has made a point of reassuring the parents that their son is safe and in no danger as long as things go his way. He used the phrase 'I promise' in the latest one, indicating he has a strong sense of honor and right and wrong. His word matters. As a profiler, I have to say I don't think this guy has any intention of harming either of his victims. That's not to say he won't snap at some point and change his mind. After all, he's enraged enough at AbaCo to have taken the drastic action of kidnapping someone. So, he does have a breaking point."

Laura made a sound of distress. "And we're

going to see it when he finds out the trial's not going to happen at all."

The call from Laura's CIA contact came in just a few minutes before five o'clock. The look of abject relief on her face said it all: they'd gotten their extension on the announcement that the AbaCo trial had been suspended.

She put down the phone and said, "He's got a firm commitment to delay twenty-four hours and a tentative agreement to postpone the announcement for up to forty-eight hours beyond that. It was the best he could do."

It wasn't perfect, but it was better than nothing. He and Laura could breathe for another few hours. Her shoulders slumped in front of him and it was all he could do not to gather her up, carry her upstairs and make love to her. Anything to escape this endless nightmare for just a few minutes. But no way would she agree to such a thing. Regretfully, he turned his attention back to figuring out something, anything, to do to help find Adam.

He said thoughtfully, "You know, the kidnapper keeps emphasizing burying AbaCo, not necessarily the trial itself. You already said it to—" he broke off sharply. Mustn't mention their extracurricular visit to Kloffman. He continued in chagrin, "You said it to me. What if, instead of testifying, I go on a media blitz to tell my story and slam AbaCo all over the airwaves? Done properly, I could probably tank the stock price and get the senior leadership fired. I could mire AbaCo in scandal so deep they'll never recover."

Laura turned around and looked up at him doubtfully. "If you do that, you'll sacrifice a shot at a legitimate trial at some future date. You'd be giving away your chance to get justice for the crimes committed against you. Maybe you just launch a campaign to overturn the sale of Spiros Shipping and get it back."

Nick shrugged. "If I get my son back,

who cares about justice or shipping compa-
nies? Even if they skate on the kidnapping
charges, you have to admit there'd be a certain justice in destroying the reputations of
AbaCo's senior leadership and wrecking the
company."

Laura winced. "How many people would
you put out of work? Do you think you're capable of destroying the business your great-
grandfather built and your entire family
poured its heart and soul into?"

Nick had to unclench his jaw to grind out,
"How can you ask that of me? Do you really
think I'm that shallow and materialistic? He's
my son. Nothing on earth is more important
to me than him."

Laura scowled back at him.

It was one thing to know they were both
just lashing out in their stress and panic, but
it was another thing entirely to stop the unreasoning fury bubbling up inside him, demanding that he yell at someone, anyone, in
his agony. He knew Laura was feeling the

exact same way. But it was still hard not to turn on her. They *had* to maintain a unified front. Work together. Adam's life depended on it.

Blackledge broke the heavy tension between them. "May I remind you that a massive manhunt is in progress as we speak? Let's not give up on the idea of finding and rescuing your son outright, shall we?"

Laura glanced over at Blackledge in chagrin. He was right. But it was so in her nature to have a plan B in case the main plan failed, and a plan C if plan B didn't work out, that she couldn't help coming up with contingencies for the crisis at hand.

The second video had put her mind a little more at ease. It was a good thing for a mother to know her child wasn't scared or in pain. And thank goodness Lisbet was still alive and with him. She'd protect Adam with her own life, Laura had no doubt. But there was still the dilemma of how to proceed, given that they weren't ultimately going to be able to meet the kidnapper's demand in a court of law.

Nick's thoughts must be running in the same vein, because he said soberly, "It would be a calculated risk to launch a media war against AbaCo. Maybe it would satisfy the kidnapper, maybe not. And if not, we'd have blown our shot at a trial that would satisfy the guy. What do you think about it, Laura?"

She looked up at him thoughtfully. "I think Agent Blackledge is right. Let's allow the manhunt to play out while we see what our… friends…can come up with now that we've got a few more days to search for Adam." She looked at him significantly. *And in the meantime, they'd meet with Kloffman.*

Nick nodded resolutely. "Done."

She touched his hand lightly, silently thanking him.

He responded, "In the mean time, how do

you feel about heading up to Washington for the night?"

She nodded and glanced over at the FBI agents within easy earshot. "You know me well. I'm starting to feel claustrophobic just sitting around here. I'd like to be close to Langley in case I have to twist some arms in person tomorrow. I'll go pack a bag for Ellie."

Nick nodded briskly. "I'll call the hotel and have them arrange for a babysitter."

Blackledge snorted. "Are you kidding? You're bringing along an FBI agent to guard your baby."

Laura glanced at Nick in chagrin. He said smoothly, "Excellent idea, Agent Blackledge. I'll call the Imperial Hotel and get us all a suite."

The FBI man nodded. "Morris, you've got kids, right?"

Agent Morris grinned. "Yes, sir. Five. I'm fully checked out on diapers."

"Perfect," Laura announced. "We'll leave in an hour."

* * *

Ms. I-can-handle-anything, I'm-totally-in-control vapor locked when it came time to choose a dress to wear to dinner. It was the darnedest thing. Laura stood in front of the hotel closet, staring at the dresses Marta had packed for her, mostly conservative business wear appropriate for a mother who was deeply concerned about her child's safety. And for the life of her, she couldn't choose one. It was as if her brain just shut down.

Nick stepped out of the bathroom, fresh from a shower, wearing dress slacks and no shirt, toweling his hair dry. He looked at her in concern from under his towel. "Everything okay?"

The man really was observant. "No," she wailed. "I can't decide what to wear."

He moved swiftly to her and gathered her into his arms. Smart man. He knew something was seriously wrong if such a little decision was hanging her up. His body was warm and humid against hers and smelled of his expensive soap.

He murmured into her hair, "You're doing great. I have no idea how you're holding it together the way you are. Just a little while longer, and we'll get him back. Courage, darling."

"I think I'm all out of courage," she whispered.

"Then borrow some of mine. Remember that Adam's happy and safe and the kidnapper has promised not to hurt him. We'll find a way to meet the kidnapper's demands. And Werner Kloffman's going to help us do that. He'll give us his files, and we'll be one step closer to getting our son back. But the first step is to pick out a dress and put it on."

Wise advice. Just take this one moment at a time, one simple task at a time.

He turned with her still in his arms to face the closet. "I've always liked you in blue. How about this one?" He pointed at an elegant, navy-blue suit dress.

"It's not very sexy," she said in a small voice.

He laughed. "Sweetheart, you could wear a burlap sack and a paper bag over your head, and I'd still find you sexy."

She sighed. "You do have a golden tongue. I don't know if you mean a word you say, but you say all the right things."

He kissed her forehead lightly. "I don't say them to anyone but you, so I must mean them."

She let him help her slip on the dress. He zipped it for her, and the perfectly tailored garment hugged her body with its slim lines. Nick left to finish dressing, and she pulled her hair back into a quick French twist. She added stockings and conservative high heels to the ensemble but stopped short of adding a pearl necklace to the outfit. She didn't want to look like her grandmother, after all. She tugged the dress's V-neck wider open and tightened her bra straps to increase the undergarment's lift. There. Definitely non-granny cleavage.

She smiled at Ellie who was playing in the middle of the big bed. "Sweetie, you do wonders for Mommy's assets."

The baby burbled back. Verbal early, Ellie was. Must be a girl-baby thing. She scooped up the infant and inhaled deeply of her fresh baby scent. "Mommy's going to go torture Daddy with this naughty dress for a few hours. It's going to be loads of fun. Be good for the nice FBI agent, okay?" She blew a raspberry against her daughter's tummy and laughed when Ellie squirmed and gave her a sweet, gum-filled smile.

Agent Morris poked his head through the open door. "Mr. Cass is ready whenever you are."

She nodded at the man. "Ellie just ate. She should be good for at least four hours. There's a bottle in the fridge just in case, and she should go down around 10:00 p.m. Order whatever you want from room service and watch whatever you want on TV." She added dryly, "And no boys in the house, please."

The agent grinned. "You forgot to ask me if I have a current CPR license and a baby-sitting certificate from an accredited after-school program."

Laura laughed. "I'm not paying you that much."

Morris looked around the plush suite. "Hey, this is the best babysitting gig I've ever landed. You and Mr. Cass have a nice evening. Ellie and me, we'll get along just fine." He patted the bulge on his right hip and added grimly, "Mr. Glock and I will see to it that nothing happens to your little princess on my watch."

Laura nodded, abruptly serious. "Thank you."

She stepped out into the living room and Nick made an appreciative sound. "You're stunning, Super Mommy."

She made a face. "I'm not feeling very

super at the moment. I feel like I'm hanging on by my fingernails."

"Well, you're doing it with style. You look fabulous."

She rolled her eyes. "We've been over this before. I'm the thirty-year-old mother of two."

"That's correct. You're everything I've ever dreamed of and more."

Her heart melted a little. It would be so easy to ignore his trespasses from the past. To fall into his beautiful blue gaze and forget everything else. *Exactly the way she had for the past year.*

Like it or not, she had to face up to the fact that their current predicament wasn't entirely Nick's fault. She'd been as guilty as he of ignoring the past and pretending that nothing bad could be lurking in that giant memory gap of his.

If she lost herself in him and his damnably magnetic charm again, she'd regret it as sure as she was standing here. Someday reality would rear its ugly head again, just like it had this time, and bite her. Who would get hurt the next time? Her? The kids? All of them?

It was time. She and Nick had to confront the past head-on and make peace with it once and for all. They had to do it for their children…no matter what the cost to the two of them.

Chapter 10

The place Kloffman had picked for their meeting was dark and quiet. The booths had tall dividers separating them and plenty of privacy. Laura sighed beside Nick as they stepped inside.

"What's wrong?" he murmured.

"Too easy a place to do surveillance. Not a good spot for a clandestine exchange."

"Really?"

"Loud, rowdy, and crowded is a better venue. It's impossible to eavesdrop more than a few feet away, there's lots of noise pollution to foul up directional microphones, and people are hard to keep track of in a big crowd."

It made sense. And she was the former spy, after all.

She continued, "Our best bet is to get in and get out of here, fast."

"We'll just order drinks, then. We'll get what we came for and leave immediately," he replied.

She nodded beside him and pasted on a pleasant smile as the maître d' approached. They were led to a booth near the back of the place, and Kloffman was already there, looking impatient. Nick smiled to himself. Typical German. If the guy wasn't five minutes early, he considered himself late.

Kloffman stood as they approached. Laura took his hands and greeted the German warmly. Quick on the uptake, Werner kissed her cheek and ushered them to the table like they were old friends. A waitress took their drink orders and left. Finally. They were alone.

Laura leaned forward and murmured past a

warm smile that kept her lips from moving in any significant way, "Do you have the files?"

"Yes, my dear, I do." He brought out a small box from under the table, gaily wrapped in hot-pink paper and tied with a wide white ribbon. A white bow nearly overwhelmed the fist-sized box.

"How delightful!" Laura exclaimed. "You shouldn't have brought me a gift. Now I feel bad for not bringing you anything."

Werner laughed back. "My wife insisted. She said you should open it when you get home."

Laura duly tucked the box beside her on the banquette. She then led the conversation deftly into a discussion of how Werner's grown children were doing, and what he'd thought of Southeast Asia, where he'd taken a recent vacation. Nick was impressed. How she knew that about the German executive, he hadn't the slightest idea. Or maybe she'd just made it up and Werner was adept at following along with her patter.

Nick forced himself not to look around the place, not to check for listeners or watchers. He leaned back, looping an arm over the back of the banquette and smiling at Laura like a proud husband enjoying his attractive and effervescent wife. It wasn't hard to act besotted with her. He *was* besotted with her.

In due course, he and Werner argued good-naturedly about who would pick up the tab for the drinks, and he ultimately let Werner pay the bill. With a promise to stay in touch and come visit Werner in Germany soon, Nick and Laura stood up to leave.

And just like that, the entire records of AbaCo's Special Cargo division for the past several years were in their possession.

Nick hailed a cab and Laura climbed in as he held the door for her. He settled in the seat beside her. "Now what?"

"When we get back to the hotel, we open his gift and see what he gave us," she answered lightly, glancing warningly at the back of the cabbie's head.

He supposed she had a point. They couldn't be too careful at this late date. He relaxed and watched the city lights pass by outside. Washington really was a lovely city, a gracefully aging lady.

Agent Morris was on his feet, gun in hand and leveled at their chests, when they walked through the door to their suite. Nick nodded his approval as the guy lowered his weapon.

"You two are back early. Everything okay?" the FBI man asked.

Laura shrugged. "I made it through cocktails, but I'm not comfortable being away from Ellie. I convinced Nick to bring me back here for a quiet dinner in our room."

Morris nodded in sympathy. "How about I go take a nap with our little princess? Then I'll be in good shape to stand watch through the night. And in the mean time, you two could probably use a little privacy."

As the agent retreated, Nick called room service and ordered dinner.

He joined Laura at the desk in the corner of

the living room as she booted up her laptop and plugged in the thumb drive she'd found inside the gift box. A long list of file names scrolled across her screen.

"How's it look?" he asked.

"If the files contain what their titles suggest they will, we've got a whole lot of dirt on AbaCo we didn't have an hour ago."

"Anything jump out at you that might have something to do with Adam's kidnapping?" he asked.

She typed quickly. "I'm going to do a sort for files created in the past year. The start date for the search will be the day you were released."

She undoubtedly didn't mean for that subtle note of blame to enter her voice, but it did. His gut twisted at the notion that his liberation was in some way the cause of Adam's predicament. He had to make it up to the boy, and to Laura. Adam *had* to be okay.

As she continued to type in what looked

like a long list of random words, he asked, "What are you doing now?"

"Setting up keywords for the computer to search for within the files. The guys at AbaCo aren't likely to run around talking about kidnapping openly. They'll use euphemisms like 'picking up a package' or 'moving perishable goods.'"

Nick snorted. He'd felt like perishable goods plenty of times, sailing around in that damned shipping container. Laura threw him an apologetic glance.

"I've also set up a sorting algorithm to copy and organize all the content on this drive. It'll take a few minutes to run." She sighed heavily. "In the meantime, I think you and I need to go over the events from immediately before your kidnapping."

He jolted in alarm. "But I don't remember—"

"Yes, but I do. I thought I'd tell you everything I can remember and see if it jogs any memories for you or if you remember anything about some detail that might be important."

Her suggestion made sense, but why did she sound so reluctant to revisit what had supposedly been a torrid and thrilling affair? "You're making me nervous. What's so terrible about our time together in Paris that you haven't told me?"

"You truly don't remember any of it?" she asked in a small voice.

"Nothing. I'm sorry."

She waved off his apology and took a deep breath. "You saved my life the night we met."

"What?" Shock poured through him. "How?"

"My CIA field partner and I were attacked and you came out of nowhere. You grabbed our elbows and told us to come with you or die. Kent shook off your hand and demanded to know who you were."

Nick frowned. "I thought you types worked alone. You had a partner?"

Unaccountably, she blushed slightly. "Certain operations were best suited for couples."

Ahh. Damn. But it wasn't like he was in any position to cast the first stone at her. He had a wife floating around in his past. Of course an extraordinary woman like Laura had other men in her life. He asked as lightly as he could manage past his abruptly hoarse throat, "Were you two a couple?"

"Were. Past tense by then. The demands of keeping our roles as coworkers and lovers separate was too much strain on the relationship."

"Why did I grab you two?"

Laura frowned. "It was late at night. It had been raining and the streets were mostly deserted. We were in the *Quartier Latin*—the Student Quarter. Lots of winding little streets and alleys. Several men had just come around a corner about a block ahead of us, and you materialized by my side. You must have come up from behind us. When Kent jumped away from you, you wrapped your arms around me and yanked me into an alley."

"Why did you come with me when your partner didn't?"

She smiled a little in recollection. "You were extremely handsome. Not many girls would mind having a man like you throw your arms around them and drag them off."

Nick frowned, scouring his mind for the slightest recollection of what she was describing. He came up blank. Frustrated he asked, "Then what happened?"

"I heard a noise in the street. Then a scuffle. Kent shouted something. It sounded like the beginning of my name. Then it cut off. And then nothing more."

"What did you and I do?"

"At the first sound of fighting, you pulled me down the alley. By the time Kent went quiet, you didn't have to pull me anymore. You had a car not far away and we drove off into the night. The rest is, as they say, history."

Misery filled her dark gaze and Nick moved quickly to embrace her. "Talk to me. What's so upsetting to you?"

"I left him, Nick. I abandoned Kent. I should have stayed and fought. Maybe the two of us could've bested whoever jumped him."

Oh, how well he knew the world of regret and self-recrimination. "Sweetheart, what's done is done. It's just as possible that the two of you would have lost that fight. Whatever fate met your partner could also have befallen you. There's no way of knowing. I assume you did your best to find out what happened to him?"

"The CIA and I turned Paris on its head looking for him. But he was just…gone. Very much like how you disappeared. He's never been seen or heard from since."

Nick frowned. "Is there any chance he was kidnapped like I was?"

She shrugged. "I suppose. We know AbaCo held more prisoners over the years than the dozen or so they've released in the past twelve months. For all I know, there are more men and women just like you still floating around in international waters where law enforcement agencies can't touch them."

"Maybe we'll find the rest of them in the files Kloffman gave us."

"God, I hope so," she muttered.

Turning his attention back to Paris, he asked, "Do you have any idea how I found you that first night or why I pulled you out of there?"

"You refused to answer any of my questions about it and just said you 'had a feeling' there might be trouble."

He grinned ruefully. "I highly doubt I was psychic back then. I had to have known something."

She sighed. "That's what I thought. But every time I brought it up, we'd end up kissing and then…well, you know. My superiors thought we might be able to develop you into an asset once we learned more about you, so they told me not to press you too hard."

It was his turn to sigh. "I do wish I could remember falling in love with you the first time. I'm immensely grateful I got to do it again."

Her arms tightened around his waist. "I'm just grateful I found you. I swore I wouldn't give up until I did."

He murmured into her hair, "And it's that same stubbornness that's going to bring Adam home to us."

"From your lips to God's ears."

He lifted her chin lightly, sealing her words with a kiss. He'd meant for it to be a simple gesture. Harmless. But instead, her arms wound around his neck, and with a sound of need in the back of her throat, she was suddenly all over him. And her desperation was all the excuse his needed to cut loose.

His arms came around her fiercely, lifting her off her feet and crushing her against him. They traded frantic kisses, tongues clashing as their hands ripped at their clothing. Never breaking the chain of heated kisses, they stumbled toward the master bedroom. He kicked the door shut with one foot as she dragged him by the open shirt toward the bed. They fell across the mattress, and his hands plunged into the deep V-neck of her dress, finding and seeking plump handfuls of female flesh. He shoved her clothing aside, his mouth fastening on one rosy peak. She arched up into him with a cry of need, filling his mouth with her bounty.

And then she was tearing at his remaining clothes, dragging his zipper down and freeing his rock-hard erection. He lifted his mouth away from her long enough to mutter, "How do you feel about three children?"

She laughed and fumbled in his back pants pocket, freeing his wallet, and fishing out the ubiquitous emergency condom inside.

He yanked her dress up and her panties down while she shoved his slacks aside and put on his protection. And then she grabbed his hips with eager hands, pulling him forward impatiently, her legs wrapping around him hungrily. He plunged into her heat, groaning at her tightness as she surged up around him.

It wasn't pretty or elegant. It was a fast and furious tangle of clothes and limbs and heavy breathing as they raced pell-mell for escape from everything to do with their real lives. It felt so good to lose himself completely in her, to sink into the pleasure of her body, to turn himself over to pure sensation, to turn off his mind completely and think of nothing at all. Just the blinding ecstasy of nerves shouting for release and the ever-more-urgent collisions of flesh on flesh as they both strained toward oblivion.

The cries started in the back of her throat, small at first, then building in intensity as her climax neared. He kissed her deeply, sucking up her pleasure hungrily. Their tongues took on the rhythmic movement of their bodies and the slick slide nearly pushed him over the edge. Her body went taut beneath his, arching up hard into him. He tore his mouth away from hers to stare down at her, reveling in the way her eyes glazed over and her breath stopped as a shattering orgasm broke over her. Her shuddering groan was the final straw. He plunged deep one last time as his own body exploded.

It was almost as if he passed out for a second. Everything went dark and peaceful and quiet, and nothing existed but shivering pleasure tearing through his body in wave after wave of exquisite, almost painfully intense, sensation.

Time lurched into motion once more. Laura was panting and her hair was a disheveled and entirely sexy mess around her face. Perspiration coated his bare chest, and somehow his shirt had gotten tangled up around his shoulders. Laura's dress was askew and her lips were pink and slightly swollen.

"We shouldn't have," she gasped.

"Why not?"

"Adam. Here we are having a good old time…wasting precious minutes we should be using to find him…so selfish…" She rolled away from him, yanking violently at her clothes, putting them back in place if not exactly to rights.

Who was she referring to when she spoke of selfishness? Him? Her? Both of them? "Sweetheart, a little emotional release isn't a bad thing. We're both stretched to the breaking point—"

She cut him off with a sharp gesture of denial.

If he knew one thing, it was how to survive. And that meant being supremely selfish sometimes. Grabbing happiness whenever and wherever he could find it, hoarding it to himself, and reliving it greedily. He tried again. "You'll be no good to Adam if you don't take care of yourself."

"I'm fine. He needs me, and I let myself be distracted…. I can't believe you went there with your son's life on the line."

"I'm sorry. But I think you're underestimating how stressed out you were. Don't you feel even a little bit better?"

"No. I feel guilty and self-indulgent. If something happens to Adam, it'll be *my* fault."

"Laura." He took her by both shoulders and forced her to look up at him. "You did not kidnap him. You are not responsible for this. Don't take guilt onto yourself that is not yours to carry."

"Easy for you to say," she snapped. "You conveniently forgot everything in your life you should feel guilty for. You've got a built-in free pass."

He pulled back sharply. So. The truth finally came out. She did resent his memory loss, and she didn't forgive him for it. He'd long suspected she harbored hidden anger about it, but she was such a damned good actress, she'd never really let on how she felt.

He understood her perspective. Really. But it wasn't as if he could do anything about it.

He was what he was, like it or leave it. And recent mind-blowing sex notwithstanding, apparently she'd rather leave it. Leave *him*.

He went cold from the inside out. It was as if he froze, every cell and fiber of his being crystallizing in an agonizingly slow spread of needle-sharp pain. The muscles of his face froze, and he couldn't make a meaningful facial expression in that moment if his life depended on it. Only his thoughts continued to function, spinning fruitlessly round and round like a car doing donuts on sheet ice.

How were they supposed to proceed from here? Either she trusted him or she didn't. Forgave him or she didn't. Accepted him— all of him, his past and his problems in- cluded—or she didn't.

The verdict was in. His attempt to make a life with her and the kids was an epic failure.

His survival instinct kicked in. Must keep busy. Give himself small jobs to do. Count the ribs in the walls of his box. Check his food and water supply. Exercise and stretch.

Press his eyes close to the small hole in one wall of the box. Keep his retinas acclimated to light. Think about the business plan for the new company he was going to start when he got out of here. Just. Keep. Moving.

Mechanically, he mumbled, "I wonder if our dinner's here yet." Take care of basic body needs first. Food. Water.

"I'm taking a shower," she announced, revulsion plain in her voice.

She wanted to scrub the feel of him off of her. The frost surrounding his heart hardened a little more, constricting painfully. He'd lost his son, and now her. The blow was almost more than he could bear. An urge to crumple to the floor, to curl up in a ball, to close his eyes and slip into the black abyss in his mind nearly overwhelmed him. He almost wished for his box. Things had been simple in there. Clear. Survive one day at a time. One sunrise to the next.

But this—this he wasn't sure he could stand.

He stood in the middle of the bedroom and

stared at nothing until he heard the shower water cut off. The sudden silence spurred him to motion and he stumbled out into the living room.

Laura emerged from the bedroom a while later. He had no idea how long it took her to dress. He pulled a chair out for her at the table their dinner had been laid upon. She sat down, silent, and he moved around to sit across from her. The rounded stainless dome over his plate had actually kept his fillet mignon lukewarm. The meat was tender and juicy. It probably tasted wonderful, but he couldn't tell. It all tasted like sawdust.

Laura ate quickly and then moved over to her computer to start cruising through the AbaCo documents. The search for Adam was all they had left between them.

He had files of his own to search. The ones he'd lifted from William Ward's desk after the attorney had been murdered. Maybe they'd have information in them that might lead to his son. Even the idea of such a project overwhelmed him right now. He needed to think more simply than that. Move to desk. Open laptop. Turn it on. Insert flash drive into USB port.

"What's that?" Laura asked suspiciously.

"The thumb drive I found in my lawyer's desk."

Her brows shot up in surprise. "I assumed you'd already looked through that and hadn't found anything worth mentioning."

He sighed. "I was avoiding it, actually. I expect there'll be information in here about my past, and I wasn't ready to face it until now."

The dishonesty of his words tore at his tongue as if it were being ripped off a frozen well handle. He still wasn't ready to face his past. But it wasn't like he had any choice. Adam's life hung in the balance, and he'd walk through the fires of Hell for his son.

Laura's gaze was dark and accusing.

The directory of files on William's secret storage device scrolled down the screen in front of him. It looked like a list of client names. Most of this stuff was probably highly confidential. He glanced through the list. Smith. Spangler. Spiros.

There he was. He clicked on his name.

A sub folder opened up and a list of files unfolded before him. He browsed the titles curiously. They mostly looked like business contracts. But on the third page of file names, one in particular caught his eye. It was a report from the same private investigator who'd been looking into the Nick Cass identity and found nothing. It was dated the day William had called and insisted Nick come to the Cape—the same day William had died. Nick abruptly felt as if he'd just been kicked in the stomach. Hard. Taking a deep breath, he clicked on the report and started to read.

"What did you find?" Laura asked from across the desk. Sometimes the degree to which she was observant made living with her damned hard. Or more to the point, made living with secrets around her damned hard.

He answered heavily, "I think I just found my prenuptial agreement with Meredith."

Chapter 11

What little breath Laura had left after the mood swings of the past two hours whooshed out of her. She felt like a washcloth that had been twisted and squeezed until every last drop of life had been wrung out of her. She was empty. Emotionally done in. Logic told her this was an extreme situation and not to make any major life decisions in the midst of the crisis. But the urge to sweep aside everything and everyone who stood between her and Adam was irresistible.

Nick began to read aloud. She exhaled carefully as he went through a ridiculously huge list of assets. Nikolas Spiros hadn't been merely rich. He'd been wealthy beyond imagining. And she had a pretty big imagination.

"Listen to this," he exclaimed. "If I die of unnatural causes, she gets nothing."

"As in zero?"

"That's correct. Not a dime. And in fact, she's required to return any jewelry, clothing, cars, homes, or cash assets accrued during the marriage to my estate."

"Wow. Trust her much, did you?"

"Apparently not."

"Sounds like you thought she was a potential black widow even before you married her," Laura responded.

Nick was frowning, too. "It does beg the question, why did I marry her in the first place if I thought it was a good possibility that she'd try to kill me for my money?"

"Were you always that mistrustful of the women you dated?"

"It was an issue wondering if women wanted me for myself or for my wealth. But at some point, you have to take a chance and go with your gut. I may have gotten it wrong with Meredith, but I got it right with you… twice."

She brushed aside the overture. Adam was her entire focus at this juncture. But the mystery of Nick's marriage to a woman he clearly thought dangerous tantalized her. Was Meredith behind either or both kidnappings after all?

The man she knew—both in Paris and now—simply wouldn't have married a woman in whom he had so little faith. Surely Nick's core personality hadn't changed that much in the past six years. "Do you have any idea how you met Meredith?" she asked.

"No, I don't."

She asked cautiously, "Would you mind if I researched your wife a little?"

His gaze was open and honest, and he answered without hesitation. "Be my guest."

Thank God. He was finally willing, not only to face his past, but to let her see it, too.

She minimized the AbaCo files and pulled up her favorite search engine. She typed rapidly.

In seconds, pictures of Nick and Meredith from the front pages of the tabloids leaped onto her screen. "Attractive woman," Laura commented.

Nick shrugged. "Beauty comes from inside a person. *You're* attractive. From what I know of her, she has the heart of a snake. She may be well-groomed, but she is *not* attractive to me."

Laura might have smiled under other circumstances. But as it was, she kept typing grimly. "She was living pretty high on the hog when you met—designer clothes, expensive hotels and spas, jewelry running into hundreds of thousands of dollars…" She typed some more. "Did you know she was collecting art? It looks like she'd bought a couple million dollars' worth by the time you two hooked up."

Nick looked about as interested as if she'd

told him the price of tea in China had gone up by a penny a pound.

Laura poked around some more, but then leaned back, perplexed. "I can't find the source of her money. She doesn't come from a wealthy background, and I'm not finding any indication she had a high-paying job. She had a high school education from an average school. No college. She wasn't a model. Several years prior to meeting you, she started tossing around the big bucks. She didn't appear to be dating any men who could've financed that sort of lifestyle. According to her tabloid appearances, she seemed to be picking up mostly good-looking toy boys and footing the bill for them."

Nick made a face. "Maybe she was a hooker."

Laura snorted. "Even high-end working girls don't pull down the kind of money she was spending. She was blowing through three to five million dollars a year."

"Was she running up a massive debt? Maybe she married me to dig herself out?"

Laura gestured with her chin toward his laptop. "Is there any record of your attorney running a background check on her? My lawyer used to run one on all the guys I dated in college, and I didn't inherit anywhere near the wealth you had."

Nick scowled. "I seem to recall William checking out my girlfriends at university, and it drove me crazy."

"Did you tell him to stop?"

He laughed. "I doubt William would have listened to me. He was the executor of my father's estate and had the power to do pretty much whatever he pleased. As I recall, he didn't think I was exactly the most responsible young man on the planet."

"Was he right?"

"Absolutely. I was in my early twenties, good-looking, smart, and too rich for my own good. Girls flocked to me, and I had no problem taking advantage of that. William kept me on a stupidly tight financial leash. Good thing he did, too. I might have blown my inheritance before I grew up and got interested in the shipping business."

"What else could Meredith have been up to that pulled in so much cash?" Laura asked thoughtfully.

"No education. No fancy job. No modeling. No prostitution. No rich boyfriend," Nick ticked off. "She was either the secret mistress of someone extremely wealthy, or she was into something illegal."

Laura spent the next several minutes looking at Meredith's travel patterns over a three-year period. She found no recurring destinations. She even cross-checked the guest lists at various hotels and resorts Meredith frequented and found no pattern of any repeating guest at the same places. Tabloid references consistently called Meredith single and on the prowl. She appeared to subscribe to the theory of a new man in her bed every night. Laura even ran Meredith's name through the various intelligence databases that she had legal—and occasionally way off the books and not so legal—access to. There were no records or even rumors of the woman being involved with anyone. Nada.

Finally, Laura announced, "If she was having a secret affair, it's so secret I can't find any hint of it. I think the crime angle is all we've got left."

"Given what Kloffman says she's into now, it seems the likeliest scenario."

Laura nodded. "Okay. Let's assume she was already dabbling in crime. She comes to you with a plan to use your shipping company to expand her activities. Do you say yes or no?"

"Emphatically no," Nick replied firmly. "I always ran a legitimate business."

Laura nodded and continued her line of reasoning. "But she doesn't take no for an answer. She figures she can seduce you and gain access to your company that way. Either she figures she can do it behind your back, or once you're married, you'll go along with what she's up to and take the money and run rather than turn in your wife."

Nick pushed his laptop aside and propped his elbows on the desk. "But what if, after we were married, I didn't want to go along with her plan for Spiros Shipping?"

Laura picked up the thread of the logic. "Then she's got to get rid of you. But because of the prenup, she'll lose all control of, and even access to, the shipping company if you die."

"So, she has me kidnapped, tosses me on one of my ships, and has it sail around indefinitely in international waters with me aboard. For all I know, I might have been the first prisoner. Maybe she got the idea for selling high-end kidnappings from me."

Laura scowled. That woman had better hope her path never crossed Laura's. On behalf of all the families of the kidnapping victims, she was going to gouge the woman's eyeballs out with her bare hands.

"Surely I suspected something before I married her, or else I wouldn't have insisted on this crazy prenup."

"Is it possible you had in mind some sort of scheme to expose what she was up to and married her to find out what exactly she was involved in? Maybe to expose who her business partners were?"

Nick stared into space for a long time. It was painful watching him try to dredge up a memory that simply wasn't there. Finally, he huffed in frustration and his gaze focused on her once more. "Yes, it's possible. But I don't remember." He added in a rush, "I wish now that I'd cooperated with all those shrinks who tried to help me remember the lost years."

Laura jolted. She'd long suspected he'd stonewalled his doctors, but to hear him say the words aloud was a shock. "Why didn't you cooperate?"

He laughed shortly. Without humor. "I knew something really bad had happened during that lost time, and I was dead certain something even worse would happen if the docs uncovered it."

She had to give the man credit. He was one fine actor to have fooled all the physicians like that. But it did raise another and more disturbing question: What else wasn't he being square with her about?

It took her a moment to pick up the dropped threads of their conversation. "Okay, so you suspected Meredith of being up to no good. Maybe she was already using your company to ship illegal somethings."

He nodded. "But she was too careful, and I couldn't find out what she'd involved Spiros in unknowingly."

"Do you think it's fair to assume you were acting nobly to protect your company?"

He nodded. "My only recollections of Spiros Shipping are fond and proud. I can't imagine doing anything to sabotage it."

"Okay. We go with noble motivations.

Would you have been willing to seduce Meredith to find out what she was up to?"

He nodded again, but slowly this time. "If my hobbies were any indication, I was a bit of a risk taker back then. I might have gotten involved with someone like her for the sake of my family's business. Hell, I might have done it purely for the thrill of playing with fire."

She tsked. "Nick, Nick. What did you get yourself into?"

"Apparently, I got myself into waters way over my head." He reached across the table to squeeze her hand apologetically. "I'm so sorry I sucked you into this mess."

Recollection of why they were having this conversation washed over her. *Adam.* His precious face, so much like his father's, swam in her mind's eye. Agony stabbed her.

A cold feeling settled in the pit of her stomach as a disturbing thought occurred to her. She frowned. "Do you think it's possible you knew who I was in Paris? Did you approach me because I was CIA and could help you take her down?"

A horrified look leaped into his eyes. "Surely not. Surely I wouldn't have used you like that. Maybe I found out you were getting too close to her and might ruin my investigation, or maybe you had come onto Meredith's radar and were in danger."

How could she have been so stupid in Paris? She'd been so swept off her feet by Nick's good looks and extraordinary charm that she'd never stopped to ask herself exactly why and how he'd blown into her life. What if it hadn't been happy coincidence at all? What if he'd been using her? Had their instant and explosive attraction been a lie? Had he really loved her at all?

Oh, God. And what about now? Had the past year been all about using her resources to hide from his enemies? About regaining his strength for another fight? Had their entire life together been a lie?

She reeled, both emotionally and physically, and actually had to grab the edge of the desk to steady herself. Nick was speaking again, and she struggled to focus on his words.

"...know what your partner was investigating? Did he maybe stumble across something having to do with Meredith's activities?"

She retreated into the mundane rather than dwell on the horror spinning through her mind right now. "We were investigating the Russian mob's activities in France. It's possible I didn't know everything Kent was doing, though. But I can find out." Using a dummy email account, she typed out a quick email to her old boss at the CIA asking if her partner might possibly have been investigating Meredith Black Spiros at the time of his disappearance. Clifton had also been Kent's supervisor. If anyone would know what Kent had been up to, it would be him. She hit the send button. Clifton's reply was almost immediate—he must be working late. Kent hadn't been working on anything else to his knowledge. No help there.

Her research on Meredith dead-ended for the moment, she turned her attention back to the AbaCo documents. Nick went back to reading legal documents from his lawyer's files.

She'd been perusing blindingly dull shipping documents and correspondence for about an hour when she sat up straight abruptly. She read the short email correspondence again—in Russian. Nope, she hadn't mistranslated it. Holy cow.

"Uhh, Nick? I know where your wife got her money."

He glanced up questioningly from his own computer.

"She worked for the Russians," Laura announced.

"What?"

"There's a message in here for her, in Russian. Kloffman made a note on the email that he didn't know what it was, but he was startled that a personal email for Meredith had accidentally made its way into AbaCo's files, and that it was in what looked like Russian. She apparently never let on to him that she speaks the language. I have to agree with Kloffman. It had to be a mistake that this got saved in an AbaCo archive."

"Can you read it?"

She smiled grimly. "I had a Russian minor in college."

"What does the email say? Is she a spy?" Nick demanded.

"I don't know. This could have come from the URS—the Russian security service—or possibly the Russian mob." She added dryly, "Not that it makes much difference one way or the other. The two organizations are firmly in bed with each other."

Nick stared. "Was she some sort of plant? A mole to get inside my company?"

"Maybe."

Or maybe Nick had made some sort of deal with the Russians and Meredith had been merely the instrument of its implementation. It was all well and good to spin Nick as the possible hero in the Paris scenario, but it was just as possible he'd instigated whatever criminal activities Spiros Shipping had gotten into. Maybe he'd been unwilling to add murder to the list and had saved her that rainy night as a selfish maneuver to protect himself. Or maybe he'd been trying to ingratiate himself with the CIA.

It was so maddening not knowing the truth! Did she dare trust him or not? By his own admission, he'd run interference on the doctors trying to discover the truth about his past. Had that, too, been a purely self-protective maneuver?

She had to believe his memory loss was real. Too many times over the past year, he'd casually reached for some memory in an unguarded moment and run into the black wall of nothingness. She'd seen the fear and frustration in his eyes when he didn't think she was looking. He hadn't been acting for her benefit in those moments, and he'd been absolutely consistent in his inability to remember even the smallest details of that time, even when he was half-asleep, distracted by the kids, or just surprised by a sudden question from her. No actor was that good.

Good guy or bad guy? Liar or victim? Who in the world was Nikolas Spiros/Nick Cass? She had to unravel the mystery fast or else their son might very well die.

She glanced up. Nick was frowning deeply, obviously trying yet again to pierce the black veil in his mind. "Anything?" she asked.

He shook his head. "How did she get away with being a spy, or at least some sort of Russian agent?"

That was an excellent question. Laura went back to her earlier computer screenshots of Meredith's childhood and early adulthood. Some or all of it could very well be faked. She studied the records carefully. If it was fake, it had been extremely well done. Which meant the URS was probably behind it.

Of course, working for the Russian government didn't exactly exclude Meredith from working for the Russian mob, too. Laura reached for her cell phone. "Let me make a few calls to Langley. I need to talk to the guys on the Russia desk about her."

Although she was no longer a CIA agent and her clearances had long been terminated, she was nonetheless considered to be a friend of the agency. In that capacity, people listened to the occasional tips she passed their way. And in return, they threw her a bone now and then. An anonymous male voice answered the line.

"Hi, my name's Laura Delaney. You can run my bona fides past Clifton Moore in the morning. He'll vouch for me. Please copy the following for immediate dissemination: I believe I have discovered a long-term Russian mole. A sparrow possibly, functioning inside and behind a major international cargo shipping company."

The man at the other end of the phone

made a sound of surprise. Over the years, there'd been a lot of rumors about the KGB's vaunted core of operatives who used sex as a potent weapon of espionage. The men had been called ravens, the women, sparrows. But the talk had been mostly rumors and urban legends.

She continued briskly, "Her name is Meredith Black Spiros. I have reason to believe she is using the resources of AbaCo Shipping to engage in much more extensive illegal activities than the Agency is currently aware of. Her financials are highly suspicious. I recommend the Agency take a closer look immediately. I'm requesting any additional information available on her. Have you got all that?"

"Yes, ma'am. What is a good phone number and email address at which we can contact you?"

"Clifton Moore knows how to get in touch with me." Laura hung up the phone.

"Are you so sure that was a good idea?"

Nick asked doubtfully. "If she's some dangerous spy, wouldn't she be really mad if you sicced the CIA on her? I mean, what if she's behind Adam's kidnapping? Lord knows, if she's connected with the Russians, she'd have access to the kind of resources to pull it off."

Laura shook her head, remembering Adam and Lisbet laughing on the floor. "Lisbet worked for a Russian family before I hired her. She speaks some Russian. She'd know if she were being held by one and would have used some sort of Russian word out of context instead of a French one."

Nick studied her intently. "Are you willing to bet our son's life on it? Because that's what you're doing."

None of her mommy-warning intuitions were firing. Was it possible that Meredith's true identity and Adam's disappearance were not related? One thing she was sure of: Whoever had Adam was out for AbaCo's blood, not Meredith's.

Nick surged up out of his chair. "You could've made a terrible mistake by calling Langley."

"I did my job," she retorted sharply.

"You're not a spy anymore. You're a mother. And you may have just endangered my son even more than he already is."

They glared daggers at each other, as much frustration glinting in his eyes as roiled in her gut. "I wasn't being impulsive or reckless," she snapped. "As a citizen, I have a duty to report a national security risk to my government."

"It's pretty arrogant of you to decide that all by yourself, don't you think? He's my son, too."

"And where were you the first five years of his life?" she shot back. She regretted the words the second they were out of her mouth, but once said, they couldn't be unsaid.

"It's not my fault I was locked in a box that whole time! I didn't know I *had* a son. And even if I did, there isn't a damned thing I could've done about it."

He was right. But he also had no idea what it had been like, having no clue where he'd gone or why he'd just disappeared like a puff of smoke from her life. In spite of her determination to find him, she had to admit—if she was being brutally honest with herself— that part of her had been furious at Nick during the long years of his absence.

She'd been left at home to wait and worry and raise her son as a single parent. To dodge the difficult questions about who and where his father was when Adam got old enough to start asking. It hadn't been easy keeping her act together, and for the first time, she admitted to herself that she'd hated Nick a little for it.

In fact, she still hated him a little for it. She knew intellectually that he'd been through no picnic himself. That five years of captivity had nearly broken him mentally, physically, and spiritually. Maybe she just wanted a little acknowledgement from him that she hadn't had an easy path to walk, either.

She was being selfish. Immature. Down-right stupid. But she was also too exhausted to keep up the Super Mommy façade any longer. She wanted Adam back, and she wanted all this crap from Nick's past to go away and leave her and the kids alone. Was that too much to ask? Was that selfish of her? Maybe. But she couldn't help it. That was how she felt.

Finally, as physical and mental exhaustion claimed her, she crawled into the big bed in their room. Nick joined her in tense silence. Thankfully there was little chance of a repeat slip between them like earlier.

She lay in the dark for long hours beside him, listening to his deep, even breathing. And everywhere her thoughts turned, she only ran into questions and more questions. Thing was, she was an answer kind of gal. If she didn't start getting some of those soon, her head was going to explode.

* * *

"Why don't you two crazy kids go out for breakfast?"

Nick glanced up at Agent Morris and smiled. "While I appreciate the sentiment, I think Laura and I would rather get straight to work finding our son."

"The FBI's doing everything in its power to find Adam. We're not exactly schlubs when it comes to that kind of thing, you know."

Nick answered smoothly, "And we appreciate all your efforts. But we can't help using all of our personal resources as well."

Morris nodded in commiseration. "If it were my son, I'd be doing the same thing. Do you need me to keep an eye on Ellie while you two run around this morning?"

"Actually, that would be incredibly helpful."

"All right, then. I'll hold down the fort here."

Laura emerged from the bedroom just then and Nick glanced up at her cautiously. He didn't blame her for being in a volatile emotional state, but frankly, he didn't have any idea what to expect from her this morning.

Frustration scored across his skin like the tines of a fork—sharp enough to hurt, but too dull to make a nice, clean cut. He was not accustomed to feeling so damned helpless. Even when he'd been at the complete mercy of his captors, he'd never succumbed to the ever-creeping sense of helplessness. He'd controlled his own schedule, tracked weather patterns, exercised, and engaged in any number of mental activities to stay sane. At least until he got so debilitated that he couldn't do it anymore. But that had only been near the end. Not long before Laura and her friends rescued him. All else aside, he'd always be grateful to her for that.

"How did you sleep?" he murmured to her.

She shrugged. Which meant she hadn't slept at all. He followed up with, "Come up with any new ideas while you were staring at the ceiling all night?"

"I've got to go to Langley this morning. I need to make sure the Agency delays the announcement about the trial like it said it would. And while I'm there, I'll find out what they've got on your wife."

Uh-oh. Meredith was "his wife" this morning. He winced and muttered, "I prefer not to think of her that way. She will be my ex-wife as quickly as my law firm can file divorce papers."

Laura merely pressed her lips together as she poured herself a cup of coffee.

"Shall I drive you?" he asked in resignation.

"If you like."

"Agent Morris has volunteered to babysit Ellie for us."

Laura turned and thanked the FBI man warmly. Okay, then. So this morning's chill was reserved for him. Nick sighed and stood up. "I'm ready to go whenever you are."

The morning traffic had mostly thinned out by the time they reached the heavily wooded

Rock Creek Parkway. In thick silence, he guided the nimble BMW along its winding curves. Without warning, the GPS screen mounted in the middle of the dashboard shattered, and his hands jerked on the steering wheel in shock.

"Shooter at six o'clock!" Laura bit out, turning in her seat while she fumbled at her purse.

No kidding. He stomped on the accelerator and glanced in his rearview mirror. Sure enough, a small round hole had appeared in his rear window, a spiderweb of cracks radiating outward from it. A silver sedan matched his acceleration behind them.

As soon as he spotted a break in the oncoming traffic, he ordered, "Hang on."

Slamming on the brakes, he yanked the hard left on the steering wheel, came off the brakes, and floored the accelerator as the Beemer screeched around in a sharp one-eighty turn. His side window shattered, showering him with tiny chunks of tempered glass. He ducked, but grimly kept his foot on the gas. As tires screeched behind him, their car roared down the Rock Creek Parkway in the opposite direction.

The BMW wove in and out of traffic, startling drivers and leaving a trail of irritated horn honking in their wake. The good news was the frightened drivers had mostly been forced to brake hard to avoid his driving tactics, and in so doing made themselves an even more difficult obstacle course for their pursuers to wind through.

It took a few minutes of entirely reckless driving on his part, but eventually, Laura announced, "I think we've lost them. Time to get off this road."

Nick took the next right turn slowly enough not to lay down any tire marks and accelerated down a side street in northwest D.C. Brick row houses flew past in a red blur. He turned a few more times, and eventually, eased off the accelerator. He guided the car west until they hit the Beltway and followed

Laura's instructions until an unobtrusive sign for CIA headquarters came into sight.

"Correct me if I'm wrong," Nick said, "But did someone just try to kill us?"

She replied dryly, "In my experience, when someone's shooting a gun at you, they generally want you dead, yes."

He grinned reluctantly.

"You just missed the turn!" Laura exclaimed.

"Think about it. No one tried to kill us until you called the CIA and told them Meredith is a Russian agent. Doesn't the timing of this morning's attack make you a little suspicious? You wanted to know if the CIA's involved with her? I think you just got your answer. Either that, or there's a leak inside your precious agency, and Meredith and AbaCo's goons found out we're on to them." And wasn't that a hell of a choice? Meredith was either a double agent herself or working with one inside the CIA.

Laura stared across the damaged car at him

in dismay. "If it's someone in the CIA, we've got to get off the road. Hide. They'll order the FBI to find us. And that bunch has massive resources for tracking fugitives." Her voice dropped into a tone of horror. "Ohmigosh. We've got to get Ellie. *Now*."

His heart began to pound. No. God, no. Not his baby girl, too.

Nick yanked out his cell phone. "Agent Morris, listen to me. You've got to get out of there. Fast. Someone just tried to kill us. Head back to the estate and we'll meet you there. And don't take new orders from anyone else. I'll explain when you get to the house. Got it?"

"Did he agree to do it?" Laura asked tightly when Nick disconnected.

"Yes."

She sagged in her seat, her face gray. She looked as close to breaking as he'd seen her since this whole mess started.

"Let's go home," he said quietly. He opted not to switch out his Beemer for a new car. It would take too much time. Right now, he just wanted to get them to the estate, surrounded by Laura's state-of-the-art security system and a houseful of hopefully untainted FBI agents, and get Ellie back under their protection.

Laura nodded wearily as he pointed the car south.

What had they stumbled into the middle of? How big was whatever conspiracy they'd uncovered? They knew for certain that someone in the CIA was in bed with AbaCo— Kloffman had confessed that to them. But did the Agency know AbaCo was being run by a Russian operative? Was the CIA being duped? Or was it using AbaCo with full knowledge of its shenanigans for the Agency's own advantage?

From what they'd learned of Meredith to date, his best guess was that the woman was playing everyone against each other and raking in piles of profits in the meantime. The question was did everyone else know what she was doing? Were they all looking the other way because they needed her to do their dirty work? Or was there some sort of sinister conspiracy to protect her and the illegal shipping she would do for anyone?

How deep into the government did the complicity go? Did it reach beyond the CIA? Into the FBI even? Was the FBI legitimately trying to find their son? Or was the whole search for Adam nothing but smoke and mirrors, a ploy to shut them up while Uncle Sam covered its tracks?

This mess was slipping away from them. And Adam was going to end up caught in the cross fire. Sick certainty of it roiled in his gut.

For that matter, Laura was slipping away from him, too. Faster than the tide rolling out on the beloved beaches of his home. She doubted him. Doubted his honesty. Doubted his motives—both in Paris and now. Not that he blamed her. The circumstantial evidence didn't look good for him. If only he could *remember.*

The doctors had told him that if his memories didn't start to spontaneously return on their own within a few months of his release, they were probably gone for good. He'd thought that was just fine until this mess blew up in his face. Now, it was coming back to haunt him in a big way.

His son was gone. His daughter was possibly in the enemy's hands. Laura hated him. His attorney had been murdered, and now someone had tried to kill him and Laura. It was as if a net had snared him, drawing tighter and tighter until he couldn't move. And even knowing full well what was closing in around him, he couldn't find a way out of the trap.

Mile by mile as he drove into Virginia, he felt Laura pulling away from him. The more time she had to think, the farther she withdrew. And there wasn't a thing he could do to stop it. He didn't remember what had happened between them in Paris or why; he had no explanations for her. And he refused to make up some glib lie. She deserved better than that from him.

Their life, their love, was unraveling before his eyes, slipping inexorably through his fingers. And no matter how hard he tried, he couldn't catch the falling threads. For the first time in his life, he felt truly helpless.

If only there were something she could *do!* This sitting and twiddling her thumbs, waiting around for some new development, was maddening to Laura. She needed some fact to uncover, some door to knock down— heck, someone to shoot.

Desperation was creeping up on her, choking her slowly but surely, and there was nothing she could do to hold it back. All of her avenues for finding Adam were drying up, and she didn't know where to turn next. Even during the long years of Nick's absence, she'd never felt this alone, this helpless, darn it. MysteryMom could use a dose of her own medicine. If only there was someone who could roll in and save her from this nightmare like she'd done for so many women before.

Her love for Nick had always been her rock, the touchstone she returned to when everything else in her life went to pieces. But now, she didn't have the slightest idea if it had ever been real. Had she built her life on a foundation of quicksand, after all?

She glanced over at him. He was staring ahead, his expression inscrutable. He was so beautiful to look at that it hurt, sometimes. And her son was a tiny carbon copy of the man. Adam reminded her so much of him that it was hard to separate her love for the two of them in her mind.

And now there was Ellie to add to the pie. She favored Laura a little more in her features, but she had Nick's dark hair and shocking blue eyes.

What had she done to her children? How

were they supposed to grow up with an enigmatic ghost for a father? Would he stick around to see them grow up, or would his dangerous world suck him away from them again, this time for good?

How was *she* supposed to survive if he left? Her whirling merry-go-round of thoughts screeched to a halt and stuck on that one. She might be furious at him for endangering their son, and she might be pushing him away for all she was worth right now, but she couldn't fathom his complete absence.

What *if* he left? The hell of it was that, for the life of her, she couldn't come up with an answer for that one. The idea of a life without Nick in it yawned before her as black and featureless as Nick's lost past.

When Nick had been gone before, people kept telling her to carry on for the sake of her son. And they were right up to a point. Even now, she knew she had to carry on for Ellie. But even she had a breaking point. And she was becoming increasingly concerned that she was reaching it. For better or worse, she loved Nick too much to survive without him. Too much to let go of him.

The two of them were headed for a crash, and there wasn't a darned thing she could do to stop this runaway train.

Chapter 12

Laura's heart was heavy as Nick approached the estate from the back entrance. He parked the damaged BMW at the far end of the garage behind the SUV Marta usually used to go shopping and run errands, and she followed him silently into the house.

"Is Agent Morris back with Ellie?" she asked with a casualness she did not feel.

"Not yet, ma'am," one of the FBI agents at the kitchen table answered.

"Any news?" she asked the men.

"No, ma'am. But Agent Blackledge wants to talk to the two of you."

Laura caught Nick's faint frown and

matched the expression. They stepped into the library and Nick asked shortly, "What's up?"

The FBI supervisor looked up from a computer. "I need you two to stay in closer touch with me. In fact, I'd prefer it if you stopped your gallivanting around altogether."

Her warning instincts went on full alert, shouting frantically at her. They weren't exactly out partying the nights away. They were trying to find their son. What was going on, here? She prevented herself from blurting the question sharply, but still asked, "Why?"

Blackledge's gaze went opaque. Unreadable. Whatever he says next is going to be a lie. "We're kicking the investigation into high gear and events are likely to move faster from here on out."

"Does that mean you have new information you think will lead you to Adam?" Nick asked with a casual calm that was completely at odds with his keen, assessing gaze.

"We have resources well beyond what I can

share with you," the FBI man answered with false warmth. "I'm sure you understand."

Okay, her warning instincts were screaming at her, now. First, the attack on them in Washington, and now this sudden evasiveness from the FBI agent in charge of Adam's recovery? She was dead certain the two were related. How deep into the U.S. government did AbaCo's tentacles reach?

She risked a look at Nick. A pleasant smile was pasted on his face, but he'd gone faintly pale. A person had to know him well to spot it, but he was as freaked out as she was. Not good. Very, very not good.

"Honey, I'm a little dizzy. Do you think you could help me upstairs?" she said wanly. "I think I need to lie down."

Nick, ever quick on the uptake, took her elbow solicitously. "You haven't been resting enough, darling. I know you're panicked, but you have to trust Agent Blackledge and his men. They're doing all they can. And if anybody can find Adam, it's the FBI."

He led her slowly from the room. As she left, she glanced out of the corner of her eye at Blackledge's turned back. His shoulders had come down from around his ears. Good. He'd bought their act.

When the bedroom door closed behind them, Nick opened his mouth to speak, but she waved him quickly to silence. He nodded, his expression grim. Instead, she said, "Do you think you could get a cold cloth for my forehead, and maybe some aspirin? I'm starting to develop a terrible headache."

He headed for the bathroom while she went to her closet and opened the safe there. It contained, in addition to the usual jewelry and back-up copies of important personal documents, an array of paraphernalia from her days as a spy. She pulled out a sensitive electronic scanner and checked their room in minute detail for any sign of bugs or cameras.

It was clean. She nodded at Nick. "As long

as we keep our voices down, we can speak freely."

Nick blurted under his breath, "What the hell's going on with Blackledge? Why the sudden stonewalling?"

"I'm afraid you were right earlier. My call to the CIA about Meredith and AbaCo has upset someone. A lot. Enough to reach into the FBI to mess with the investigation of Adam's kidnapping."

Nick spoke thoughtfully, "I don't think Blackledge was involved in it before. He was legitimately trying to find Adam until this morning. I think this interference comes from above his pay grade."

"I have to agree with you."

"That means we can pretty much kiss off getting any significant help from the U.S. government from here on out with finding Adam. We're on our own."

The sense of isolation she'd been feeling before slammed into her even more force-fully. Tears, hot and infuriating because she had no time for them, filled her eyes. She swore at herself under her breath.

Nick was there in an instant, his arms strong around her. "We'll figure this out together. We're both smart and experienced at these sort of games. Besides, I promised Adam I'd keep him safe from the bad man."

"I'm not so sure the bad man has him," Laura mumbled against his chest.

Nick froze, arrested by the observation. "You know, that's a very good point."

She looked up from where she was smearing mascara on his white dress shirt. "How's that?"

"I think we may be on the same side as Adam's kidnapper in this whole mess. I wouldn't go so far as to say he's done us a favor by pulling our son out of harm's way, but there may be an element of truth to that. If the kidnapper's not associated with the CIA, FBI, or Meredith, he may be safer with the kidnapper right now."

"Oh my god," she breathed in horror. "The FBI has Ellie."

She couldn't help it. She started to shake, and then to cry. Not her baby, too. Her legs collapsed, but Nick caught her against him. He bent down, scooped her legs out from underneath her and carried her over to a big armchair by the window. He sat down, cuddling her against his chest like a baby, herself.

No matter how bad things were between them, they were both worried parents. They would always have that in common. And right now, she wasn't strong enough to turn down his emotional support.

Nick murmured soothingly, "As long as we play along with them, I can't imagine they'll keep her from us. We just have to pretend that everything's okay until Agent Morris gets here with her." His eyes lit up. "In fact, I have an idea. Blackledge is a single guy, right?"

Laura nodded.

Nick grinned. "Even better." He dug out his cell phone and dialed quickly. "Agent Blackledge. It's Nick Cass. Do you have an ETA on Agent Morris and our daughter? My wife is getting…uncomfortable…you know, nursing mother…to pump or not to pump…"

She smiled in spite of herself at the awkward sputtering suddenly coming from the other end of the phone.

"Twenty minutes? Thanks," Nick said. "If you could have someone bring her up right away…"

More sputtering. Nick hung up. "There you go. Twenty minutes."

To pass the time, Laura climbed out of Nick's disturbingly comfortable lap to check her email—the private one she hadn't told the FBI about. A familiar name caught her eye as she scrolled down through various junk mails to it. "I got a message from Clifton Moore."

Nick tensed. "What does he have to say?"

Foreboding filled her as she opened the short message and scanned it rapidly.

Federal prosecutor will announce suspension of trial in a press conference at 8:00 a.m. tomorrow. Be sure to put eyes on it.

"Not so soon!" she gasped.

"What?" Nick moved quickly to her side and read the message for himself. He swore quietly. "We're out of time. We've got to *do* something."

She added tightly, "'Eyes on' is an old code phrase between Clifton and me. He's telling me my investigation is compromised from inside the Agency. We can't trust the CIA."

"We sure as hell can't trust the FBI, either," Nick replied.

She looked up at him in dismay as the totality of their isolation struck her. "We're completely on our own. If we're going to find

Adam and rescue him, it has to be now. We have until 8:00 a.m. tomorrow morning."

"It's time for Daddy Finders Inc. to become Adam Finders Inc. To heck with the government. We'll find him ourselves."

Panic rolled through her, a wild storm riding a wind of despair. "I can't do this," she whispered.

"Maybe not alone," Nick replied firmly. "But together we can do this. We're both highly intelligent and extremely motivated. Between the two of us, we have massive resources outside the U.S. government. The first order of business is to find somewhere safe to leave Ellie tonight." He ticked off the requirements on his fingers. "She needs to be out of the house, with someone we trust, and whom the government won't know to look for."

Laura nodded, mopping tears from her eyes that threatened to spill down her cheeks. Nick was right. She couldn't fall apart now. Adam needed her. Needed *them*. And goodness knew, they couldn't drag Ellie all over the countryside when they went after Adam. Memory of that awful chase through the Cape Cod woods with men shooting at them and Ellie screaming her head off flashed through her mind.

She announced suddenly, "I know just the person. Emily Holtz's mother lives not far from here. Emily's the woman who helped rescue you from the ship."

Nick nodded. "I remember her well."

"Her mother, Doris, is as fierce as a lioness when it comes to protecting her cubs. She was the woman in the safe room with Adam the night we rescued you and brought you here. She protected Adam when your kidnapper tried to recover you."

"Sounds perfect. Now we just have to figure out where Adam is."

He made it sound so easy. She'd been wracking her brains for days as to how to identify and find Adam's kidnapper to no avail. How to begin? A comment Nick had made earlier came back to her. Laura said thoughtfully, "You said before that Adam's kidnapper is on the same side we are. Let's follow that logic for a moment. Expand on what you meant by that."

Nick answered, "The kidnapper's mad at AbaCo. He wants to see them buried. Why? What did AbaCo do to him? If we could figure that out, it might give us a clue as to who he is."

Laura looked up into his eyes hopefully and continued the logic. "He knows AbaCo's been doing things that can get the company in serious trouble. Which means he's either in the Special Cargo division or has done work for it."

"Why is he taking action now? Why not earlier? Has he seen something that goes beyond what he can stand morally without taking action?"

"It probably isn't smuggled stuff in boxes that's got him so riled up. AbaCo's been doing that for years. Whatever goaded him to action is something new. Something appalling to anyone with a smidgen of conscience."

Nick added grimly, "Humans locked away in boxes for years on end might make him mad enough to act. And it might explain why he chose me specifically to put the screws to. He figures I'm as mad about that as he is. He can trust me to tear AbaCo apart with the vigor he thinks the company deserves."

Laura continued eagerly, "So instead of searching the entire AbaCo employee roster for fired employees, we should look for someone who's left the Special Cargo division recently under any circumstances. Maybe retirement or just quitting. The FBI's investigation of fired employees might not have been broad enough."

Nick rose as well. "And we just happen to have the Special Cargo division's complete personnel roster for the past few years, compliments of our friend Kloffman."

She raced over to her laptop and reached for the keyboard.

Nick said sharply, "Are you sure the guys downstairs won't see what you're doing on that?"

"Good point. Let me deactivate my wireless access and throw up a couple of extra security protocols."

"Maybe you should wait until Ellie's safely with us," he suggested gently.

She lifted her hands away from the computer, frustrated. "Waiting is so hard," she whispered.

"I got pretty good at waiting in my box," Nick murmured. "Come here."

As conflicted as she was about him, she wasn't about to pick a fight with him now. Adam's life depended on the two of them setting aside their differences and working together. Reluctantly, she sank into his lap and had to admit it felt shockingly nice.

He murmured, "I used to think about the vacation I would take when I was freed. I would imagine it down to the smallest detail.

Where shall we go as a family when we're all back together?"

A family. Oh, how she liked the sound of that. If only it could be. She turned her attention to his question and replied, "You have to ask? We have small children. There's only one place on Earth to take them."

Nick laughed. "Orlando, here we come." He continued, "Shall we wait until Ellie's a little older or go right away?"

"Both, I think."

He nodded encouragingly. "Now you're getting the hang of it. What will we do first with the kids?"

They spent the next several minutes planning the details of their vacation. Although it did help her pass the time while they waited for Ellie's return, a little voice in the back of her head wondered if any of them would ever get to take the trip. She mustn't think that way!

A knock sounded on their door. Laura leaped out of Nick's arms and threw the portal open. A smiling Agent Morris stood there with a bundle of pink fuzzy blanket in his arms. It was all Laura could do not to fling herself forward and tear her daughter away from the guy. As it was, a sob shook her as the man handed her daughter over.

Nick thanked the agent quietly and closed the door as she retreated to their bed and unwrapped her daughter to perform a count of every last finger and toe. The infant was perfectly fine and thankfully hungry.

She nursed Ellie while Nick activated additional security protocols and opened a search algorithm on her laptop following her instructions. The three of them sprawled on the bed together, with the computer between them. Over the baby's dark head, she helped him build a mini-program to search the Special Cargo division's detailed personnel files.

Nick hit the enter key. The computer would eliminate all females, all non-French-speaking men, and all deceased employees in the Special Cargo Division. Then it would search for employees who'd left the division recently for any reason, rank ordering them according to when they'd left AbaCo. In a few minutes, a list of names scrolled down the screen.

Nick commented, "Unless our guy was some sort of contract longshoreman who didn't actually work for AbaCo, I'd lay odds our kidnapper's on this list."

She nodded resolutely. "Now we just have to figure out where all these guys are. The one we can't account for is our kidnapper."

"Easy as pie," Nick retorted. "We'll both work on it, and it'll go faster."

It didn't turn out to be quite that simple, however. The two of them spent the rest of the afternoon working on their respective laptops, hunting down the whereabouts of dozens of former and current AbaCo employees. His knowledge of the company's personnel record system turned out to be invaluable. Laura hacked into AbaCo's current Human Resources records, and he navigated rapidly to the address list used to mail various pension checks and insurance information to former employees. By eliminating those people who lived outside of North America, they removed over half the suspects from their list.

At about dinner time, someone knocked on their door. They hastily closed their computers and Nick opened the panel. A female FBI agent stood there. "Would you like us to send up some food?" she asked.

"Yes. That would be perfect," Nick murmured, turning on the charm. Laura watched in amusement as the agent blushed. She knew the feeling. The guy was impossible to resist. "Any new information?" Nick asked.

The agent stiffened fractionally and threw a glance in Laura's direction. "No, sir. I'm sorry."

Nick shut the door and pressed his ear to it, presumably to listen to the woman's retreating footsteps. He turned sharply. "She was lying."

Amused, Laura asked, "You're good at telling when women are lying to you?"

He answered sourly, "It comes with the territory when you're a reasonably eligible bachelor."

She laughed lightly. She had no trouble imagining the legions of women who must've thrown themselves at him over the years. More seriously, she asked, "Do you think she suspected anything?"

"No. You looked appropriately wan and distressed when she checked you out."

Laura snorted. "You're not the only good actor in this family."

He rolled his eyes at her, but accepted the compliment. If, indeed, it was a compliment at all. They traded a look of complete understanding. The two of them were cut from the exact same cloth. They did what it took to get the job done, and neither of them took life lying down. They went out and got what they wanted and didn't wait around for things to come to them. And right now, they wanted their son back.

She said quietly, "Shall we press on with our investigation?"

He nodded and gestured for her to precede him back to the table and their laptops.

"I think it's time to add a few more parameters to our sorting program," she announced.

"Like what?"

"People who are living on the east coast of the United States."

"We may exclude the kidnapper with those parameters. For example, the guy could live in California but have traveled here for the express purpose of kidnapping Adam."

Laura replied thoughtfully, "Setting up the logistics of a successful kidnapping takes time. The guy had to prepare a hideout, lay in supplies, figure out how to get into this house. I think he's been in this area for some time."

Nick nodded. "Your logic is sound."

"We're running out of time. We're going to have to take a few chances, follow our guts, and hope we're right."

He replied soberly, "I'd bet my life on your gut instincts."

"All right then. Let's finish this thing."

"Thank God," he replied fervently. "I can't stand waiting around anymore."

She texted Doris to ask if the woman would watch Ellie while Nick modified the search program. Doris responded almost immediately that she'd be delighted to babysit Ellie. As Laura was replying that they'd be at her home sometime later in the evening, Nick's computer beeped.

Laura got up and moved around to see what their revised search-and-sort program had turned up. Five names blinked on his screen. Now they were talking. That was a much more manageable list of suspects.

Nick piped up. "Can you check and see if any of these five remaining guys have bought land nearby in the last few years?"

She nodded, liking his logic. They knew from the videos that Adam was being held at a cabin of some kind, likely surrounded by woods to explain Adam's leaf collection. She ran a search and came up with nothing, however.

Nick frowned. "Can you search farther back? Maybe our kidnapper bought land and held it for a while before he built a cabin on it. Or maybe he's had it for a long time."

Again, frustratingly nothing. Her head was starting to throb. This line of research had to pan out. They didn't *have* anything else.

Nick spoke again. "How about searching county tax records for the surnames of these guys? Maybe the land's been in the family for a long time."

She frowned. "Not every county has digitalized its tax records. But it's worth a try."

They got a list of hits, maybe twenty properties in all. She dragged the addresses to a map program and a series of pinpoints popped up on a map of the mid-Atlantic region. She commented, "One of the leaves in Adam's collection came from a bush that grows well near salt air. So let's assume he's near the Atlantic coast. That leaves us with these four locations."

They tried several more search programs, and nothing they did could narrow down which property was the likely hiding place of Adam's kidnapper. There was no help for it. They were going to have to check out all four. It was going to be a long night.

As she packed an overnight bag for her daughter, Laura's maternal urges protested at leaving Ellie with Doris. But she knew it to be the best thing. She had no right to endanger an infant, and furthermore, tonight's activity would require stealth. And as she knew from personal experience, crying babies did *not* qualify.

She and Nick waited until Ellie had nursed and was deeply asleep to put their plan into motion. Laura loaded Ellie's spare baby bag with pistols, ammunition, and a small pair of night vision goggles. She opened the safe in her closet and threw in nearly a hundred thousand dollars in cash, too. It was mostly hundred-dollar bills bundled into five-thousand-dollar stacks. In her experience, when bribing someone—like a kidnapper—cold, hard cash had a much more visceral and powerful impact than a check or electronic wire transfer.

She snuck down the back staircase to the kitchen with a sleeping Ellie in her arms. Right about now, Nick should be making a rueful request to Agent Blackledge to be allowed to go to the store and get tampons for Laura. She'd predicted that none of the all-male FBI team on duty tonight would volunteer to run the errand for him. From her perch in the shadows a few steps above the kitchen, she vaguely heard Nick grousing about three women living in a house this size and not managing to have a tampon among them. Grinning to herself, she told Marta what she and Nick were up to and slipped quickly into the darkened garage.

Nick joined her in a few moments. In keeping with the errand guise, Laura and Ellie laid down in the cramped backseat of the hybrid car the staff usually used for small errands.

"Any problems?" she murmured as the car backed quietly out of the garage, its electric motor ghostly silent.

"Nope. Just the word tampon terrified them all into catatonia," he chortled.

"Works every time on bachelors," she declared as she installed Ellie's car seat and tightened the straps holding it in place. She eased the baby into the carrier and breathed a sigh of relief when the infant didn't wake.

"Then I guess I'm not a bachelor anymore," he commented. "Female stuff doesn't scare me. Good thing, too, now that I have a daughter."

Did that mean he was planning to stick around for his kids' lives, then? The vacation to Disney World wasn't merely an exercise in mental distraction? Her initial reaction was relief, but hard on its heels came doubt. Could she trust him to follow through? Would he breeze in and out of their lives when it was convenient for him? Throw some money at the kids to buy their love and then take off again? Or would he be there for the long haul? For the doctor's visits and homework and myriad decisions that came with raising a child? Would he be there for her to lean on? To talk over parental concerns with? Did she dare share the burden with him and risk yet another disappointment?

The drive to Doris's house didn't take long. The older woman was thrilled to have a baby to spoil rotten, and her husband looked satisfyingly grim and confident when Laura relayed that there might be a threat to Ellie's safety if anyone found out the baby was here with them. Nick approved of the well-oiled shotgun Doris's husband pulled out and leaned against the wall inside the front door.

While Doris cooed at Ellie and pronounced her the cutest baby ever, Laura looked stricken. Nick put a comforting arm around her shoulders. "She'll be fine, darling. Tonight, Adam needs us."

He was right. With a last kiss on Ellie's forehead, Laura turned away from her daughter. "Let's do this," she announced soberly.

Nick nodded back equally soberly, his hand straying to the hip of his jacket, where she knew a pistol was concealed. She sincerely hoped it didn't come to that.

Chapter 13

Nick drove. Once they were alone, the research done, a plan of action in place, the temporary truce between them evaporated. Just like that, all the questions about their relationship circled them like vultures, waiting for the death of their love. Not yet. They had to rescue Adam first. Then the rest of it could fall to pieces. Thankfully, the act of steering the car along increasingly narrow and rural roads was calming. It distracted him from the mistrustful look in Laura's eyes, from the way she pulled back slightly whenever he reached toward her. He stared at the dark ribbon of asphalt before him bleakly. He'd lost everything and everyone in his life once before and survived it. A vision of Adam laughing at race cars flying across the play-room taunted him. Ellie's baby burbles as she snuggled close to him. Laura's face, trans-ported in ecstasy as they made love—

Nope. It would kill him this time.

"What can I do to make things right be-tween us?" he finally asked into the heavy silence between them.

Laura glanced over at him, startled. She answered slowly, "How am I supposed to trust you when you've kept so many secrets from me?"

"The only secrets I'm keeping from you now are the ones I can't remember. I'd tell them all to you if I knew what they were," he replied in frustration.

She shrugged. "It's not enough. I need to know the children and I will be safe from whatever or whoever else lurks in your past."

"It's not like your past is entirely free of dangers, either," he retorted. "Life is never a certain thing. You have to take it as it comes, for better or worse."

She made a sound. He couldn't tell if it was distress or disgust. "I don't recall promising any for better or worse with you."

"I'd have married you months ago, but I didn't know if I was already married or not. The only reason I didn't propose was because I was afraid to become a bigamist."

"Then why didn't you find out?" she snapped. "You knew your real name. A simple search on the internet would've revealed whether or not you were married."

"The only thing I knew for sure was that stirring up my past would be dangerous. And it turns out I was right. I knew the best and only way to make sure you and the children were safe was to lay low. And I was right about that, too."

Laura was silent beside him, but the turbulence of her thoughts buffeted him.

"I love you," he declared. "You say you

love me. Why does it have to be any more complicated than that?"

"Because it's not enough to love someone. A long-term relationship takes more than that."

"Like what?"

"Trust. Friendship. Openness. Respect."

"Haven't we had all of those this past year?"

She exhaled hard. "And were any of them real? Did you trust me enough to tell me who you really are? Were you open with me about what you do remember of your past? Did you respect me enough to tell me there might be dangerous secrets in your past?"

"I was trying to protect you and the children! Doesn't that count for anything?"

"And look how well you did at that," she replied with a hint of bitterness in her voice.

Her words were a scalpel slicing into his heart. She was right. He'd failed them all. Adam was in mortal danger, their daughter was hidden with a stranger, and Laura was on the verge of falling apart. He had to make it right. But how? If she wouldn't give him a chance, what was he to do?

The one thing he wasn't going to do was give up. He'd fight with every breath in his body to keep his children safe and win back the woman he loved. No matter how long it took or what he had to do. He gripped the steering wheel with renewed resolve. There *had* to be a way.

They approached the first cabin on foot, creeping through the woods in taut silence until they were able to peer in the windows cautiously. The tiny building turned out to be deserted. A quick look through the filthy glass panes revealed a thick layer of undisturbed dust over everything in the structure's interior. No one had been here for months.

They drove for another hour of strained silence to the second cabin. As they neared the isolated road that, according to the GPS, dead-ended at its front door, he turned off the headlights and guided the car slowly through the darkness. It coasted forward in near total silence, only the crunch of gravel under the tires disturbing the night.

"Stop here, and turn the car around," Laura instructed. "We'll go the rest of the way on foot."

He nodded and jockeyed the car back and forth, turning it to face the way they'd come on the narrow, one-lane road. No doubt she was setting them up for a fast getaway if things went bad. Always thinking several steps ahead, Laura was. He wondered if it was trained habit or intuition that led her to make the suggestion.

He had to shove his door open through a tangle of brambles and weeds. Thorns caught at his legs, and he picked his way carefully through the dangerous mass, stomping it down as he went in anticipation of his return. An apt metaphor for his entire life, right now—jumping on thorny problems in a futile effort to keep from being hopelessly snared by them.

"Did Super Mommy bring the diaper bag of doom?" he murmured.

Laura smiled reluctantly as she pulled night vision goggles out of said diaper bag and donned them. They made her look buglike. "I'll take point."

He fell in behind her, amused at the abrupt shift from Super Mommy to Super Spy. He'd been on a half-dozen photo safaris in Africa, and creeping through the woods at night like this reminded him strongly of trying to get close-up pictures of lions in the Serengeti.

Laura stopped and pointed ahead. He looked forward over her shoulder and spotted the vague outline of a man-made structure ahead. "There it is," she breathed.

Stealthy creeping came naturally to him as they eased toward the cabin. Laura paused in the shadow of a broad, bushy juniper and he moved up close behind her. They were looking at the back of the cabin. A small porch stuck out, one side of it dominated by a large, stacked woodpile. On each side of it was a window. Both windows were boarded over with plywood, and no light crept around the edges of the boards.

Laura took a hard look around the clearing, and then signaled him forward. They sidled up to the porch. Nick took each step one at a time, gently easing his weight onto each foot to minimize creaking. Laura did the same. She gestured for him to press his ear to the door while she watched his back. He nodded his understanding.

The wood was rough and cold against his ear. Holding his breath, he concentrated hard. He thought he heard a scrape inside. A shuffle of sound. His adrenaline spiked hard, and abruptly his heart pounded like a bass drum in his ear.

"Someone's home," he mouthed silently.

Laura nodded, the movement jerky as if she was tense, too. She eased down off the porch by slow degrees. It was nearly impossible to restrain his impatience behind her. But he understood the drill. Ten minutes of slow stealth now was better by a mile than an injured child—or worse.

They backed into the woods to crouch behind a stand of brush and confer quietly.

"Now what?" he asked.

For the first time he could ever remember, he saw indecision on Laura's face. The sight tore at him as little else could. A mother terrified for her child's safety was a terrible thing to see. He reached out to squeeze her hand.

"We have to make contact with the kidnapper, but we can't freak him out. We don't want to scare him into doing something rash."

Nick nodded. "Sounds reasonable."

"But I don't know how to do this. I know how to perform surveillance on secure locations, how to break and enter practically anywhere, but I have no clue how to initiate a conversation."

"How about we knock on the front door like we did with Kloffman?" Nick suggested.

Laura blinked. "You think that would work?"

"I think it would if you do it. A woman's voice is a lot less intimidating than a man's. And if he recognizes you, he knows you would never do anything to endanger your son."

She nodded, thinking hard. "I'd have to make the approach alone. Unarmed."

Alarm ripped through him. "Now wait a minute. Let's not get carried away, here. I don't want anything bad to happen to you."

She gave him a sad little smile. "Something bad already has. My son's been taken from me."

Granted. Still, the idea of risking her life, too, appalled him.

"Have you got any better ideas?" she whispered.

They had no phone number, no email, no other less-direct method of talking to whoever was inside that cabin. "I guess you're knocking on the door," Nick allowed reluctantly. "But be careful."

It was her turn to squeeze his hand. "Count on it. And hey. For all we know, this isn't the right place. Some hunter out here for a vacation may open that door."

A tiny part of him hoped that was true for Laura's sake. But mostly he hoped she was wrong. Time was running out on them to find their son.

Laura took a deep breath. She couldn't ever remember being this scared—not in her career as a spy, not when she'd gone into labor with her first child, not even when she'd executed the daring rescue of a prisoner who turned out to be Nick. She shook from head to foot and couldn't seem to control her knees properly.

All she had to do was walk across that little clearing, knock on the door, somehow gain the trust of the kidnapper, convince him she and Nick were on his side, and inquire politely as to the return of their son. What could be easier?

Unfortunately, her training permitted her to think up a thousand things that could go wrong with that simple little plan, many of which ended with Adam's death and/or hers.

"If it feels bad, back out," Nick whispered. "Trust your instincts. They've never led you wrong."

Hah. If only. She'd followed her instinct to trust Nick in Paris and had lost her partner because of it. She'd followed her instincts not to push Nick about his past, and look where that had gotten all of them.

She rose to her feet and handed over her pistol to him. The diaper bag she kept with her. If nothing else, maybe she could use the cash inside it to buy Adam's release.

"The diaper bag is the perfect touch," Nick nodded. "It disguises Super Spy perfectly as Super Mommy."

If only she truly were either one of those alter egos. Maybe they wouldn't be in this mess. She was beyond tired and scared and simply doing what she had to do for her son. And after all, wasn't that what all mommies did every day?

"Here I go," she muttered.

"I love you. Be strong," Nick murmured back.

Right. Strong. For Adam. She squared her shoulders and stepped into the clearing.

Since she was planning on announcing her presence anyway, she didn't make any attempt at stealth until she reached the porch. Out of long habit, she eased up the steps so they wouldn't creak. This was it.

She dared not stop to think about it or she might very well chicken out. She raised a fist and knocked quietly on the front door. The faint noises from the other side of the panel stopped abruptly and entirely.

"Hello!" she called out quietly. "It's Laura Delaney. I'm alone and I'm not armed. I'd like to talk to you about what you know about AbaCo. I think we might be able to help each other."

The pause on the other side of the door stretched out. She waited. And waited.

Oh, yeah. She and Nick had definitely found the right place. Elation frosted the edges of the tension gripping her.

Finally, a noise sounded just on the other side of the door. Perhaps a floorboard creaking.

"I have a diaper bag with me," she said carefully. "I'm going to set it down beside me on the porch. I'm clasping my hands behind my head. I won't move, I promise. If you'd like to search me and the bag, that's fine."

Another long pause. But this time, it was broken by the sound of a bolt opening. Her knees all but gave out from under her. *Please, God, let Adam be on the other side of that door.*

The door opened an inch. No surprise, the barrel of a shotgun poked out first. And then an eye. Its owner showed a sliver of iron-gray hair and rough, tanned skin.

A gruff voice ordered, "Step back from the door."

She did as ordered.

"Now open the bag. Tilt it so I can see into it."

She knelt slowly and unzipped the pink, quilted bag.

A low whistle came from inside the cabin. "Whatchya planning to do with all that cash?"

"Give it to you if you want it."

The door opened wide to reveal a short, burly man. He looked to be in maybe his mid-sixties, with a grizzled gray stubble covering his jaw. He wore a flannel shirt over massive shoulders with the sleeves rolled up to show forearms corded in muscle. Nick had been right, after all. This guy had been a longshoreman—she'd bet her life on it. She'd also bet he'd seen something on AbaCo's ships he couldn't live with.

He took a step forward and patted her down with awkward, but thorough, hands. He muttered an apology as he handled her more private places.

"Do you want me to dump out the money so you can see there's nothing dangerous underneath it?" she asked.

"Naw, you're not that dumb." He gazed sharply around the clearing, no doubt looking for a trick. "Get inside," he said roughly.

She stepped into the cabin's living area and looked around quickly. No sign of Adam. Her heart thudded to her feet. Had she and Nick been wrong about this place? Was she wasting her time here?

Her host raised his voice and called, "You can come out."

The bedroom door opened cautiously, and two pairs of eyes, one high and one low, peered out. The door panel flew open and a small, dark-haired projectile launched itself at her. "Mommmmmeeeeeeee!"

Tears were streaming down her face by

the time Adam flung himself into her arms, nearly knocking her over. He clutched her neck until she almost choked, and she didn't care in the least. She hugged him back as hard as she could, and he finally squirmed in protest. She loosened her grip a tiny bit, but not much.

"I knew you'd find us!" he babbled. "This is Joe, and he's been really nice. He said you and Daddy were helping him and would come for me when the bad man was beaten. Did you win? Is Daddy okay?"

She made eye contact with the older man over Adam's head. "That's what I'm here to talk with Joe about." Her gaze shifted to Lisbet, who'd stepped into the room more sedately than the boy.

"Are you all right?" Laura asked the nanny.

"Yes. Joe's been a perfect host. We're both fine."

"I can't thank you enough for taking care of Adam," Laura tried to say calmly. Except the words provoked a new rush of tears down her cheeks.

"I treated him as I would my own son, ma'am."

Laura nodded, too choked up to say more.

"Took you long enough to find us," Joe rumbled. He set the diaper bag down on the kitchen table. "Didn't you bring any help with you? I was counting on that."

Huh? Laura stared at the man, bemused.

"You don't think this thing with AbaCo is over, do you?" he snorted. "They don't give up that easy. You of all people should know that."

"What are you talking about?" she asked in alarm.

"You led their goons to us, of course."

She frowned. "We weren't followed. We made sure of it."

Joe pounced on that. "We who? Who's out there?"

"Nick's in the woods. It's just the two of us."

"Damn. No FBI? No cops?" Joe demanded.

He sounds disappointed! "I don't under-stand."

"You better get your fella in here. We need to talk," Joe said cryptically. As she stared, he waved an impatient hand. "Go on. Go get him. I'll wait."

Still carrying Adam, who was attached to her like a leech—and that was just fine with her; she didn't feel like letting go of him for a good long time, either—she headed for the front door.

She stepped onto the porch and called out, "Nick. It's okay. You can come in, now."

His tall form materialized out of the trees. He strode forward, then broke into a jog, and then into a run. He bounded onto the front porch and wrapped both her and Adam in a rib-cracking hug. He buried his face in her hair, and she felt the shudder of a sob wrack his body against hers. Adam's grip shifted from her to Nick, but she didn't begrudge the two of them the hug.

"Daddy! I *knew* you'd come for me. I

missed you. I got more leaves for my album. And Joe showed me how to tie knots and build a fire and all kinds of cool stuff. Will you take me camping when we get home?"

Laughter replaced Nick's silent relief in shaking him. "Sure, buddy."

"Y'all want to bring the love fest inside?" Joe said from the doorway. "We gotta talk. And if I don't miss my guess, we ain't got long."

Nick frowned and glanced down at her.

"He thinks AbaCo has followed us. He's disappointed that we didn't bring the cavalry along."

They stepped inside and Nick closed the door behind them, asking grimly, "Did you tell him we think the cavalry's been infiltrated by AbaCo?"

"We haven't gotten to that part, yet," she answered ruefully.

"What're you two talking about?" Joe blurted.

"We think a few individuals in the CIA and the FBI work for AbaCo."

"Come again?" the older man demanded.

Reluctantly, Laura set Adam down. "Do you think you could go get your leaf album for us? Mommy and Daddy need to talk to Joe for a minute. And maybe the two of you should pack your things."

Lisbet nodded in silent understanding of the unspoken request to keep Adam out of earshot and took him by the hand.

Laura followed the men over to the rough wood table in the corner and sat down in the chair Nick held for her.

"What's up?" Joe asked shortly.

She leaned forward and asked gently, "Are we correct in guessing that you don't like AbaCo any more than we do?"

"Those bastards are killing folks. Locking 'em in boxes till they die and then tossing them overboard like trash. I don't care how bad a thing a man done, nobody deserves that."

They'd been spot-on in their assessment of Adam's kidnapper. She made eye contact with Nick and he nodded back.

She leaned forward. "As you anticipated, your kidnapping Adam spurred the two of us to turn over a few rocks with AbaCo's name on them. It turns out the person or persons running AbaCo are a front for a Russian operation. We don't know if they're Russian intelligence or Russian mob, but either way, AbaCo's doing their dirty work."

Nick picked up the thread. "It turns out they've got agents inside our government. When Laura and I poked in the wrong places, they tried to kill us."

She added, "And they've pulled strings to get the AbaCo trial called off. That will be announced at a press conference in the morning."

Predictably, Joe surged up out of his seat, swearing furiously, and paced the small room in agitation.

"But all is not lost," Nick explained quickly.

"In fact, this may work to our advantage. We can take our accusations to the media now, without the trial restricting what we can say. And Laura and I have collected a ton of damning data on AbaCo." She watched as Nick's gaze went black and genuinely furious. "We can bury those sorry bastards so deep they'll never come up for air. I swear to you, I will take them down."

Joe shook his head. "You don't understand. You have no idea how powerful these people are. How ruthless. They'll kill us all. You were supposed to bring an army with you to get the boy. Enough force to get us out of here alive and into protective custody while the Feds catch AbaCo's thugs who were sent here to silence us and prove they're up to no good."

Laura jolted. "Is that what this is about? You need protection from AbaCo? All you had to do was ask us. We'd have given it to you."

"You ain't big enough to take these guys. Hell, they messed up the U.S. government."

She frowned. "Not the entire government. I still know plenty of people whom I trust completely. People who can make you disappear. Give you a new identity. You'll be completely safe."

Joe snorted. "Like the U.S. Marshals are gonna be immune to these guys if they can get inside the CIA and the FBI? Besides, I'm a felon, now. The Feds would never help me."

The man had a point. Several, in fact.

Nick studied the older man intently. She tried to guess where Nick's thoughts were heading.

"So, here's the deal," Nick finally announced bluntly. "We owe you one for pulling Adam out of the middle of this mess and keeping him safe while we investigated AbaCo. And there's no law saying we have to press charges against you for kidnapping. What do you want from us?"

Joe looked startled. "You ain't mad at me?"

Nick shrugged. "You scared the hell out of us and nearly killed Laura when she found out Adam was missing. But you did protect him whether you meant to or not."

Laura gave Nick an approving look. He was making allies with Joe. Putting the three of them squarely on the same side of the fight.

Joe sat back down at the table. "The way I figure it, AbaCo's thugs are on their way here now if they're not already outside."

"How's that?" Laura asked sharply.

"Of course they followed you. They know how good you are at finding lost stuff. Any idiot knows you'd go after your own kid like a madwoman. Of course, you're gonna find him. All they gotta do is bug your house, track your cars and wait for you to lead them to me."

"Why are you so important to them, Joe? What do you know?"

"It ain't what I know. It's what I got."

"And what's that?"

"Video. And not just any video. I was a security technician on a couple of AbaCo's big container ships based out of the Paris office. What with pirates and all, you'd be surprised how high-tech security is on those ships. Almost as good as your house, ma'am. Took me a few weeks to figure that system out."

Nick leaned forward eagerly. "What *have* you got?"

Joe grinned broadly. "I got your ever-lovin' wife on tape bringing you down to the container ship, *Veronique*, and telling the boys to lock you up an' never let you out. She's some piece of work, that woman."

Nick lurched in his seat. "You're kidding."

"Nope. She was with a bunch of Russkies. Talkin' Russian. But see, my first job was on a Russian oil tanker and I *govoreet* me a little po russkie."

Satisfaction surged through Laura. If Joe was telling the truth, that footage would be enough to break not only AbaCo, but Nick's wife. Startled, Laura realized that was actually jealousy roiling around in her gut, purring in satisfaction that Meredith Black was about to go down in flames. "How does AbaCo know you've got the tape?" Laura asked.

"They inventory the hard copies every few days. They're read-only—takes special equipment to burn copies—so I had to take the original with me when I left. They've been trying to find me ever since."

"Have you got copies of these videos now?" Laura asked the older man.

He nodded. "Had 'em made before I snatched your boy. But who's gonna listen to a guy like me? I'm a nobody. An' I figure AbaCo'd take me out long before I convinced anyone to take me serious. But you two. You're all rich and educated and got fancy connections. Folks'll listen to you straight away. I had to make sure you testified against them bastards."

Sadly, he was probably right.

"If you'll hand over a copy of that tape to me," Laura said earnestly, "I swear to you we'll make sure the right people see it."

Joe started to speak, but raised his hand abruptly, signaling them to be silent. Laura went on full alert. What had he heard? She'd been so focused on the implications of Joe's evidence she hadn't been listening carefully.

The older man got up and moved toward the front window. For a husky man, he moved quietly. Joe reached for the curtain to peek out and murmured over his shoulder, "Turn off the lights in here, and turn on the bedroom light so whoever's out there will think we're moving within the house and not suspicious of noise outside."

Nick did as the man ordered. Laura moved to the left-hand window, and Joe took the right one while Nick went to the back door to peer out.

"Report," Laura called out quietly.

"I think I see a couple of guys off to the southwest a bit," Joe muttered.

"I've got at least one on my left," Laura said.

"Either they're better than I am or no one's back here," Nick replied quietly.

"I told you they'd track your car. Looks like I was right. We gotta go," Joe grunted. "Get Lisbet and the boy."

Laura lurched. "We don't know who's out there. How many people are there? Are they armed? Here to help us?"

Joe scowled. "Don't be stupid. Them's AbaCo's men out there. His wife's flunkies." Joe jerked a thumb in Nick's direction.

"I'm fairly certain I married her in order to trap her into revealing her schemes," Nick replied a shade defensively. "I have no recollection of her, and believe me, I'm divorcing her as fast as humanly possible when we get home."

Laura thought fast. Worst-case scenario, Joe was exactly right. And given how the last few days had been going, she was inclined to expect the worst case. They needed an escape plan. Clearly, charging out the front door with her son and putting him in the middle of a firefight was out of the question. They had to go out the back and pray it wasn't a trap.

"Our car's out the back and through the trees maybe a quarter-mile away. It's parked on a dirt road that runs north-south. Do you know it, Joe?"

"Yup. Long ways to go with shooters chasing a person."

"We could use a diversion," Nick commented.

"We don't have the resources to mount one," she replied grimly.

Joe piped up. "We got this cabin. What say we make a fireball of it?"

It could work. Particularly if they took out a couple of the people currently lurking outside, too.

Laura stepped away from the window and poked her head into the bedroom. "Lisbet. Adam. Put on the darkest clothing you have with you. Quickly. Leave everything else behind."

Nick was already yanking open kitchen cabinets looking for supplies.

"Don't bother," Joe bit out. "I got nothing like you need. I knew a little kid would be here. I took out the dangerous cleaning supplies and the like."

While the mommy part of her was grateful for his consideration for Adam's safety, the spy within her lamented the lack of good household chemicals for improvising a bomb. Hmm. A bomb…

She had an idea. "Joe, have you got an electric fan, by any chance?"

"Yeah, actually. This place ain't got air-conditioning, and it can get a mite stuffy in the afternoon."

"I need it. Quickly."

The older man nodded and disappeared into the bedroom.

She raced to the front door and rummaged in the diaper bag. "Any movement out back?" she asked Nick tersely.

"Nope."

"They're probably doing the same thing we are. Trying to figure out how to get inside and take us all down."

Nick retorted bitterly, "Yeah, but they'll bring in commandos wielding automatic weapons and it'll be lights-out for us."

He was right. If they didn't get moving soon, this confrontation was going to be over before it began. They needed to even the odds. Fast. She fumbled in her pocket, pulled out her cell phone and dialed rapidly.

"What're you doing?" Nick blurted.

"Calling in the cavalry."

"But—"

"Not the CIA or the FBI. The local sheriff."

A female voice spoke in her ear.

"9-1-1. What's your emergency?"

"There are a bunch of men outside my place." She gave the woman the address quickly. "They've got guns and a rope tied into a noose. I think it's the Ku Klux Klan. They're coming to lynch me. Hurry!"

Laura stuffed the phone in her pocket.

"The KKK?" Nick asked doubtfully.

"It was the most inflammatory thing I could think of. No lawman wants somebody lynched on his watch. The sheriff will call in every deputy he's got and probably every one in the next county over while he's at it. There'll be a half dozen men here in minutes and fifty guys with shotguns here in a half hour. And they'll know these woods."

Nick grinned as Joe stepped into the living room carrying an old-style floor fan, the round kind that oscillated from side to side. Perfect.

Laura nodded. "I need string or twine if you have it, and a manilla envelope."

"String I got. But I don't mail nothing from here."

She eyed a high shelf beside the front door. "That's okay. I can improvise." Heck, her whole crazy idea was a massive improvisation.

Lisbet and Adam stepped into the room.

Laura pulled a small jar of petroleum jelly and a plastic bag of cotton balls out of the diaper bag. "I need the two of you to mix these together as thoroughly as you can."

They set to work and she turned to Nick. "I need you to rig a string to the front door. When AbaCo's people open it, we'll need to knock over this can of baby formula." Thank God she'd never gotten around to pulling the sample can from the hospital out of the bag and had been in too big of a hurry earlier today to take it out.

Nick frowned, and she explained. "Non-dairy creamer is extremely flammable when it's dispersed in air as a cloud of powder. Ellie's baby formula is largely made of the same stuff."

Joe started to chuckle. "I worked at a grain elevator when I was a kid. We lived in fear of the dust from wheat or corn catching on fire. Would've blown the elevator sky high."

Laura nodded. "Same principle. We'll set

up this electric fan under that shelf. When AbaCo's guys open the front door, Nick's string will dump the can of baby formula down on the fan, which should disperse the formula in a cloud throughout this room."

Nick added, "And then we use the cotton balls and petroleum jelly to provide a fire to light the stuff, and kaboom—"

Laura grinned as his eyes lit up.

"—Super Mommy saves the day," Nick finished.

"That's the idea," she muttered as she positioned the electric fan. "How's that cotton coming?"

"Done, ma'am," Lisbet answered.

Laura pulled out one of Ellie's bottles and quickly stuffed the petroleum jelly soaked cotton balls inside. She bit the end off a nipple and pulled some of the cotton out the tip. "Voila. One non-dousable candle to light off our explosion."

Nick frowned. "Will it be hot enough to ignite the powder?"

Joe answered for her. "Hell, yeah. The slightest open flame around flour dust will set the stuff off."

Nick and Laura finished setting up their trap, and in a few minutes, it was ready to go. She would have loved to test the string on the door, but they didn't dare. They'd get one shot at this thing.

Joe checked out the back door one last time and gave Laura a thumbs-up just as Lisbet announced from one of the front windows, "I think I see someone moving out there. It looks like he's coming this way."

"Time to go," Nick announced grimly. "I'll carry Adam. How do you feel about piggy-backing with me, son? Can you hang on if I run really fast?"

Adam nodded, his eyes big and dark with fear. The child was far too perceptive for his own good sometimes. He knew they were in trouble.

While Joe, Lisbet, Nick and Adam headed for the back door, Laura took one last peek out the front window. A shadow slid from one tree to another right at the edge of the small clearing, no more than fifty feet from the house. Yup, whoever was out there was on the move.

She carefully lit the baby-bottle candle with a match. It gave off a bright, steady flame. The thing should stay lit for at least an hour. Although she doubted it would have to burn for more than a few minutes, given how close those people outside were. She raced for the back of the tiny cabin.

"Okay," Nick murmured. "From here on out, we move slow and silent."

There were nods all around as he eased open the door. Crouching low, he moved out into the dark. Joe and Lisbet followed and Laura brought up the rear, closing and locking the door quietly behind her.

Laura picked up a twig off the porch and jammed it into the key hole, breaking it off inside the lock. There. Now no one could pick this lock and gain entrance from this direction, limiting them to the front door and their trap. Super Mommy had done all she could to buy them an escape.

Chapter 14

Nick forced himself to breathe slowly, inhaling and exhaling on a steady three count. But it was damned hard to stay calm out here in the dark, all exposed like this. The fifty feet or so to the nearest trees seemed like a thousand miles as he eased one foot after another forward slowly, doing his best not to shuffle any leaves.

Each little noise from someone in the group made him wince, but there was nothing they could do for it. It wasn't like anyone besides Laura was a trained operative. The pistol clutched in his right hand felt heavy and foreign all of a sudden. He'd shot on target ranges before, and was even a half-decent skeet shooter. But the idea of gunning down another human being rattled him.

He clenched his jaw grimly. He'd do whatever it took to keep his son and his woman safe. Even if that meant killing someone.

Laura moved off to the left a bit, and Joe slid off to the right a little ways. Nick squinted into the darkness, trying to remember which trees he and Laura had come from between before. They couldn't afford to miss the car by much.

Lisbet stumbled slightly in front of him and crunched loudly in a pile of dead leaves. Laura gestured sharply with her hand. Even not knowing any fancy hand signals, it was clear she wanted them to stop and get down. Nick dropped onto his haunches. Adam's feet must've touched the ground, because the child's weight around his neck suddenly eased. Nick reached back to pat his son reassuringly on the shoulder.

Laura was crawling now, and Lisbet imitated her employer. Nick duckwalked awkwardly, unwilling to commit to being on his hands-and-knees and unable to protect Adam quickly if need be.

Joe moved farther off to the right and was first to reach a stand of brush. His bulky silhouette disappeared from sight. Then Lisbet slipped behind a tree trunk. And finally, tree branches closed in around him and Adam. They were far from safe, but he felt better with someplace to hide.

Ka-boom! Boom!

Bright white lit the forest around them like day as a wave of heat slammed into his back. The propane tank beside the cabin must've blown, too. Adam cried out in terror and buried his face against the back of Nick's neck.

"Run!" Laura screamed.

Nick spared one glance over his shoulder and saw a half-dozen weapon-toting men streaming around the flaming remains of the cabin. He turned and ran for his and

Adam's life. He'd hate to see how many men would've come after them were it not for the explosion. Flaming bits of debris began to rain down around him, sizzling as they hit damp leaves. Hot embers on his face felt like needles stabbing him, but he ignored them and just kept running.

A gunshot exploded off to their right. Crap. That sounded like Joe's voice grunting in pain. Was he hit? It wasn't like Nick could stop and check on the guy. Adam's arms tightened even more around his neck. *Hang on, son.*

Nick caught up to Lisbet, who waved him to go ahead of her. The young woman was fast, but not very good at seeing and dodging tree branches and brambles. Not that he was much better. He was just willing to slam into and through any obstacles in his path at this point.

"This way," a female voice panted off to his left.

Laura. He veered toward her.

"Joe?" she gasped as he fell in beside her.

"Haven't seen him," Nick grunted back.

"We need that video."

"We can't stop for him," he retorted.

She didn't answer, but merely turned even more to the left. He followed in grim silence, glad that it sounded like Lisbet was keeping up with him leading the way.

When Laura screeched to a halt seconds later, he barely managed not to slam into her. Lisbet did slam into him. Adam let out an *oomph* that was all too audible in the sudden silence.

Laura signaled something. She pointed at her eyes then out into the woods and then held up three fingers. Three men off to their right, maybe? The pistol in his hand crept up into a firing position. He peered into the trees and shadows desperately. As much as he didn't want anyone to be out there, he almost hoped he'd spot someone so he could shoot them.

Laura held up four fingers. Then five. He

didn't need to see the distress lining her face to know they were in serious trouble. They were out of distractions, and as best he could tell, they weren't even close to the car, yet. Too bad they couldn't just pay these guys off to go away. Pay…

Crouching, he slid over beside Laura. She looked at him questioningly, and he pointed at the diaper bag flung over her shoulder. Frowning, she handed it to him. He reached inside quickly and pulled out a bundle of hundred-dollar bills, sliding off the paper ring holding it together. Quickly, he scattered the bills on the ground around them.

Laura smiled briefly and got into the act, yanking out handfuls of cash. They started moving again, sliding slowly from shadow to shadow, spreading handfuls of bills all around them.

He didn't actually expect their pursuers to abandon the chase and go on a money hunt, but perhaps the incongruous sight of thousands of dollars in cash lying on the ground and clinging to leaves and branches would at least give the men pause. And they were playing a game of seconds right now.

The money ran out all too soon, and Laura took off running again. He and Lisbet followed.

The women were panting nearly as hard as he was. The woods stretched on interminably before them with no sign of that dirt road and their vehicle. Had they gone the wrong direction? Missed the car entirely?

His thighs and lungs were burning, and Adam was starting to feel like he weighed a hundred pounds. Not that Nick minded. He'd have gladly carried his son if he weighed a thousand pounds.

Without warning, a sandy track opened up before them. The road. Praise the Lord.

Laura paused, looking right and left, and took off running to the left. The footing was firm and free of obstacles, and her stride lengthened. Nick stretched out his long legs into a full run. Lisbet was falling behind a little, but he couldn't stop for her any more than he could for Joe. His first priority was to get his son out of here safely.

He thought he recognized a clump of brambles and bushes from before. They were getting close to the car, now.

And that was when the apparition rose up in front of them, standing in the middle of the road, an automatic weapon pointed directly at them. Laura pulled up, breathing hard, and he did the same. Lisbet stopped just behind him, and he felt the woman's hands go around Adam's waist, preparing to grab the boy and take off with him if necessary. If they lived through this night, he was going to make that nanny a very rich woman for her loyalty to Adam.

"My God," Laura breathed. "Kent? Is that you?"

Kent? Her old CIA partner? The one who'd disappeared in Paris the night he and Laura met? Nick peered into the darkness. A shock of recognition rolled through him. He'd seen this guy before. In Paris. Six years ago. A flash of a darkened street, wreathed in shadows not unlike these ones, came to him.

Nick didn't know if he was more staggered by the fact that he'd remembered something from the lost years, or the fact that he suddenly and certainly knew exactly why he'd been in that alley in Paris. Nick had found out that a young, beautiful CIA agent's partner had defected to the Russians and was setting her up for kidnapping. *Laura had been the target that night in Paris.* He'd taken it upon himself to save her because it would be a rush to play James Bond and because he thought she was hot.

"Hi, Laura. You're looking good," the Russian double-agent said casually.

"I thought you were dead," she exclaimed. "I'm so glad you're alive. Where have you been?"

"Long story."

Nick snorted. "Is that what they call treason these days? A long story?"

Laura glanced at him in shock and dawning comprehension. She looked back at her old partner in dismay. "How could you? We were lovers. Friends."

Kent shrugged. "The money was a hell of a lot better on the other side of the fence."

"You sold Nick out for money?" she asked in burgeoning outrage.

Nick corrected gently, "He sold you out, not me. You were the target that night, Laura. Kent and Meredith were going to kill you."

She glanced over at him in horror, then over at her old partner. "No. We were going to meet an informant. And the guy turned on us. Kidnapped you."

"I was kidnapped because I knew too much. If it weren't for that crazy prenup, they'd have just killed me. Isn't that right, Kent?" Nick asked. He continued gently, "Kent works for Meredith. Tell her. Laura deserves that much from you. After all, you betrayed a woman who loved you."

"You loved me?" Kent asked sadly.

"Yes," she half whispered. "I did."

Nick interjected. "Look. We've got a small child with us. Let him and Laura go and you can have me."

"No!" Laura cried out, staring at him, aghast. "The two of you have to leave. I couldn't live with losing either of you."

Something big crashed out of the trees behind them just then, and Nick and Laura whirled simultaneously to face this new threat.

Nick grunted as a bloody Joe all but fell into him. He caught the man and barely managed to keep his feet under the man's weight. Lisbet rushed forward to wedge a shoulder under Joe's armpit. Adam started to cry and Nick shushed him. The child buried his face against Nick's neck and continued to shake with now-silent sobs.

"They're coming," Joe gasped. "Did what I could. Go."

"We've got a small problem," Nick murmured to the older man. "Laura's old partner is between us and the car and pointing a big gun at us."

Laura was speaking again, her voice low and reasonable. "Let us go for old time's sake, Kent."

"Why should I?"

"You owe me one. I loved you, and I know you loved me at least a little. And Lord knows, you owe Nick one after locking him in a box for five years."

Kent frowned.

Nick added, pitching his voice to be calm and soothing, "He's just a boy. Let Adam go and we won't kill you."

The former spy seemed to consider that.

"Do you have children of your own?" Nick asked.

Kent shook his head in the negative.

Vividly aware that a whole bunch of bad guys would burst out of the trees any second and shoot them all, Nick explained with desperate calm, "You see, Laura and I are parents. We'll both die without a second thought to protect our son. And we both have weapons. As soon as you fire yours, we're both going to fire ours at you. You'll kill one of us, but you won't get us both before the survivor takes you out. Frankly, Kent, that's a trade I can live with because my son walks away alive and with one parent. How 'bout you, darling?"

She nodded resolutely beside him. "Yup. I'm good with that. Besides, these woods are swarming with law enforcement. You'll never get away from here if you fire your gun and draw them all with the noise."

Kent's weapon wavered.

Crashing noises and shouting came from the trees close by.

"It's now or never," Laura muttered under her breath.

"Let's go," Nick replied grimly.

The two of them started walking forward. When Kent didn't immediately shoot them, they picked up their pace. Broke into a jog.

And then raced past the man, who took off in the other direction.

Nick spotted the outline of the car ahead.

Gunshots erupted behind them. Maybe the law enforcement types Laura had just lied about had, indeed, arrived. Ducking instinctively, Nick dived for the car. He shoved Adam in the backseat. Lisbet piled in after him and Laura pushed Joe in the other side.

Nick glanced up in time to see a figure in black racing toward them. For the second time in as many minutes, he recognized the face bearing down on him. The *female* face. Of his wife. Meredith Black-Spiros—criminal, traitor, and bitch. The person who had not only made his life hell for five years, but who had *threatened his son*. He could forgive all the rest. But not that.

Without hesitating, he swung his pistol to bear on her.

Meredith made eye contact with him as she pointed a wicked looking semiautomatic weapon in his direction. She grinned, a disdainful expression that said she knew full well he didn't have what it took to kill her.

Quickly taking aim at the middle of her chest, he double-tapped the trigger. The impact of flying lead slammed Meredith backward. She looked down at the wet stain blossoming on her chest in stunned disbelief and back up at him. For good measure, he sent two more rounds into her torso.

"In the immortal words of Arnold Schwarznegger," Nick snarled, "consider this a divorce."

Meredith's legs folded and she crumpled to the ground.

Nick spun, jumped into the driver's seat and punched the ignition button, Laura leaped in and, hanging out the window partway, fired her weapon at someone behind them.

"Gun!" she shouted at Nick holding out her free hand.

He passed her his weapon and she continued rapid firing out the window.

Nick stomped on the accelerator and the vehicle jumped forward. The Prius wasn't exactly a Formula One race car, but in a few seconds it was still faster than a bunch of guys running on foot. Between shots, Laura tossed her empty pistol into the backseat, and Lisbet dug out a spare clip from the bottom of the diaper bag. Joe slammed the new clip into the weapon and passed it forward to Laura when Nick's pistol clicked on empty.

The accelerating car bumped wildly and careened around a corner, finally getting up a good head of steam. The sound of gunfire retreated abruptly into the distance behind them. In a few more seconds, only the sound of the car's gasoline engine whining disturbed the sudden silence.

He drove a few minutes in tense silence while everyone else watched out the back window for pursuit.

Finally, Laura said tentatively, "I think we did it."

He glanced over at her, and the two of them

traded looks of mutual relief and triumph. They had their son back. Their family was safe. *Their family.* God, he liked the thought of that.

"Uhh, sir, I think we'd better find a hospital rather quickly. Joe's bleeding quite a lot back here," Lisbet announced.

Adam wailed at that. "Uncle Joe, don't die! I never had an uncle before."

Laura stabbed at the car's GPS system and gave Nick tense instructions to the nearest hospital while Lisbet performed what first aid she could in the backseat. No ambulance ever drove so fast, and perhaps no other Prius, as Nick coaxed every last ounce of power out of the hybrid engine.

Eventually, the bright lights of a small hospital came into view. Laura had already been on the phone requesting that medics meet them at the door. Nick spotted several nurses and doctors waiting as they pulled up.

The trauma team whisked an unconscious Joe out of the back of the car onto a stretcher and then away into the bowels of the emergency room. Adam cried softly in Lisbet's arms.

"They'll do everything they can for him, buddy," Nick assured his son gently.

The three adults and Adam trailed inside the waiting room and Laura headed for the admissions desk. "You need to call the police immediately," she told the attendant. "A whole bunch of men just tried to kill us. That's how our friend got shot. They'll be here soon with big guns."

Panic lit the woman's face and she snatched up a telephone and began babbling into it.

Nick put an arm around Laura's shoulder. "You do have a way of evoking strong reactions in people."

Smiling a little, she gazed up at him. "Do I do that to you?"

"You always have. Always will."

She turned into him, leaning her forehead against his chest. "I like the sound of that."

They stood together like that for a long

moment, and he savored the rightness of her in his arms. No doubt about it, this woman was his entire world.

"Were you really willing to die for Adam?" she asked in a small voice.

"You even have to ask? Of course. He and you and Ellie are my family. The three of you are my whole world. I'd die for any of you. I *love* you." By that he meant all of them, but she was bright. She'd get that. "Laura, love is about all the things you said it is: trust and openness and respect. But it's also about sacrifice and protectiveness and taking care of those you love. Love has many, many forms of expression."

She went still against him. And by slow degrees, she finally relaxed in his arms. "You really don't remember Paris?"

"Funny that. Seeing Kent jogged a brief memory for me of the night we met. Enough to know he'd sold you out and was working with Meredith."

She jolted and pulled back to stare at him.

"If I got that back, maybe I can get more." He shrugged. "I'm willing to try if you're willing to wait for the truth before you condemn me and throw in the towel on us."

She frowned thoughtfully and he took that as a hopeful sign. At least she hadn't rejected the offer outright.

Several police cars streamed into the parking lot just then, light and sirens screaming. Laura stepped away from him to go brief the police.

It was a long night. They had to answer questions from the police for hours. Doris and Marta got calls to let them know all was well. Joe survived surgery to remove three bullets from his gut, but faced a long recovery. It went without question that he'd come back to the estate with them for that. After all, Adam had never had an uncle.

Laura was dozing in Nick's arms the next morning when an all-news channel announced that the trial of AbaCo Shipping had been suspended by federal prosecutors on grounds of national security. He woke up Laura to catch the end of the announcement, although it was moot at this point. Adam was safe and asleep with Lisbet in one of the examining rooms under police guard.

Nick was surprised, though, when the newscaster continued, "In other news, wealthy socialite, Meredith Black-Spiros was found dead last night in Virginia. The circumstances of her death are being withheld by police pending an investigation."

He jolted. "Will they send me to jail for killing her?"

"She pointed her weapon at you, and you had every reason to believe she would fire it. Trust me, it was self-defense all the way. Joe and Lisbet and I will all testify to it. No worries." She reached up to smooth the furrows from between his brows. Slowly, his clenched neck and shoulder muscles unwound.

Laura glanced up at him out of the corner of her eye. "What are your plans now that she's dead?"

Nick shifted so he could look down fully at her. "To marry you as soon as possible if you'll have me. After that, I'd like to work with those doctors of yours—cooperatively this time—to see if I can recover any more of my memories for you, so you'll know without a shadow of a doubt that I always loved you and only you."

She was silent for a long time, and then she said slowly, "I don't need a psychiatrist to extract that information from your mind for me to know it's true. I've known it deep down in my gut all along. I was just hurt and scared and worried about Adam. Can you forgive me for doubting you?"

"Truly?" he breathed.

"Pinkie swear," she avowed solemnly.

The explosion of joy in his gut was so forceful it hurt. Laughing, he answered, "Darling, there's nothing to forgive. I'm the one who needs forgiveness. I swear, everything I did, good, bad, or stupid, was to protect you and the children."

"I believe you. Only a man who loves his family would offer to sacrifice himself to save them like you did last night."

She leaned up to kiss him, and as always, he lost himself in her the moment their lips met. She was everything he'd ever wanted and more. How blessed was he to have found her not once, but twice in a lifetime?

"Uhh, Laura?" he mumbled against her mouth.

"Hmm?" she mumbled back, not breaking the addictive contact.

"You didn't answer my question."

"What question would that be?"

"Will you marry me?"

She leaned back to smile up at him. "I thought you'd *never* ask."

For some reason, his heart was pounding and his face felt like it was on fire. "Is that a yes?"

She laughed softly. "Of course, it's a yes. I was a goner from the moment you stepped out of that alley and saved my life."

His arms tightened around her. "You've got that all wrong. You saved me that night. You've saved me over and over, in fact. How can I ever repay you?"

"Love me and the children for the rest of our lives."

"And our grandchildren's and great-grandchildren's lives," he promised.

She sighed blissfully and relaxed in his arms. "What are we going to do with ourselves now that our family is all safe and Super Mommy can hang up her diaper bag?"

Smiling, he replied, "That's one heck of a diaper bag I've got to live up to. I was thinking about getting my shipping company back and cleaning up its act. I'll teach Adam how to run it when the times comes."

"And Ellie," Laura added firmly. "This is an equal-opportunity family."

Nick smiled broadly. "I wouldn't have it any other way." He pondered with no small wonder what kind of woman Ellie was going to grow into with a woman like Laura to raise her. "What about you, darling? What do you want to do next?"

"First, I want to pick up Ellie and take my whole family home. Then I was thinking about going back into the daddy-finding business. It's a whole lot safer than tangling with kidnappers and double agents."

Thank goodness. He'd had all the excitement he could handle for a few decades.

Laura's cell phone rang and she dug it out. "Huh. It's Clifton Moore." She spoke to her former boss briefly. "You're sure about that?" A pause. "Okay then. Thanks."

Nick waited until she disconnected to ask, "What was that about?"

"His people have found Meredith's mole in the CIA. He was Kent's old college roommate, and he rolled over on her man in the FBI. They're both in custody and singing like canaries. She was Russian mob. It looks like we smoked out a whole network of arms dealers, human traffickers, and smugglers."

"Not a bad day's work, Mrs. Spiros," he murmured.

"Mmm, I like the sound of that." She snuggled more closely against him.

"Get used to it, darling. You're going to be hearing it for the rest of your very long and happy life."

"I love you, Nick."

He was never going to get tired of hearing that. Even if she spent a hundred years saying it to him every day, those words were always going to make him feel like the luckiest guy alive. And just maybe he was.

Epilogue

Laura glanced up from her computer as Nick entered her office. "Hi. How was the meeting today?"

"Couldn't have gone better. You're looking at the brand-new chairman of the board of AbaCo Shipping. And as my first act in the job, I made a motion to change the name of the company back to Spiros Shipping."

"Did it pass?" she asked eagerly.

"Unanimously." He came over to her desk chair and leaned down to nibble on her ear. Ripples of pleasure spiraled outward from her earlobe. If he wasn't careful, they were going to have that third child they'd been talking about soon rather than later.

He whispered in her ear, his lips moving deliciously against it, "Then, in another unanimous vote, the board appointed me CEO."

Beaming, she threw her arms around his neck and kissed him soundly. "Oh, Nick. That's wonderful."

"Are you busy this afternoon?" he asked, glancing significantly at her. Deliberately misunderstanding his intent in asking, she answered casually, "I got an email from Todd Blackledge. I was just replying to it."

"What did our favorite FBI agent have to say?"

"He's been reassigned to the New Orleans office. He got promoted to agent-in-charge of something or other. At any rate, he likes it down there. He mentioned a little problem he's having, though."

Nick massaged her neck under her hair just the way she liked it. She was going to be putty in his hands if he kept that up for much longer. She murmured, "Apparently, there have been several suspicious disappearances of babies down there."

"Is he investigating it?"

"There's no case, formerly. The local police are handling it. But he was wondering if maybe I could look into it. Unofficially, of course. See if I can turn anything up."

"I thought your thing was tracking down missing dads."

She frowned. "Yes, but these women's babies are gone. Many of them are single moms with no family or resources to track their children down. I know exactly how panicked and helpless they're feeling right now."

Nick's gaze met hers soberly. Neither of them would ever forget what it was like not to know where their son was or if he was safe. "I think you should help them."

"It might mean more time working for me. More time away from you and the children."

"I know you. If you might help a mother get her baby back, you won't be able to live with yourself if you don't try."

She tugged on his tie, bringing his mouth down to hers, and whispered against his lips, "Thank you."

"I can think of a better way for you to thank me—"

"Mommy! Daddy! You'll never believe what we saw at the zoo today!" Adam burst into the office with Uncle Joe in tow. The older man had fully recovered from his gunshot wounds and taken to his duties as bodyguard to Adam and Ellie like a fish to water. Lisbet followed more sedately, carrying a sleepy but smiling Ellie.

Nick scooped up Adam, exclaiming, "Pee-Yaw! You smell like an elephant. You need a bath!"

"With bubbles?" Adam asked eagerly. Even Ellie perked up at that suggestion.

Laura laughed and followed the entire entourage upstairs. "Now you've gone and done it, Nick. We'll be mopping up the mess for hours."

"Ahh, but you're so good at cleaning up messes," he retorted, laughing.

He wasn't too bad, himself. Between the two of them, they'd managed to put not only their family, but their romance, back together, stronger than ever. Laura stepped into the bathroom and laughed as a fistful of bubbles came flying her way.

"Oh, it's on now," she said, laughing.

Yup. Life didn't get any better than this.

* * * * *